S0-AEB-671

"You look…amazing." His voice could have melted ice.

Romy felt amazing. Doubly so as she saw herself reflected in the dark pools of his eyes. Her embroidered bodice followed the contours of her bust snugly, giving her a boost in all the right places. The skirt fell in luxurious fawn folds to her ankles. Clint's green eyes swept leisurely up the length of her.

Her pulse thrummed in places she'd never guessed she had one. "You look…dangerous. But good." How could it feel as if he was touching her when they were a meter apart? So much for keeping a safe distance.

"I'm feeling a bit dangerous right now," he said. "Maybe we should get going?"

She turned back to the car but his large hand came out and wrapped around hers.

"I'd like to drive," he said. "And before you protest, no, this is not a guy thing. I just… Cinderella should not have to drive herself to the ball."

Oh. She swallowed past the sudden knot in her throat. Even in three-inch heels she still had to tip her head to look at him.

"Will you let me drive, Romy?"

He said *drive* as if he meant *make love to you*. In a voice of pure molten lava. Her body trembled. No way was she capable of arguing.

Stop it!

Clint's focus dropped to where she'd smoothed the fabric tightly against her thighs as his capable, tanned hands turned the ignition.

Sixty kilometers to drive.

Oh my…

Dear Reader,

Prior to planning this book I had no cause to learn about the men and women of Australia's Special Services—their history, their goals and the extraordinary way they put their lives on hold for their country. On as little as thirty minutes' notice to active duty they've had to walk out of their children's birthday parties or leave sleeping wives in the middle of the night to head off to some war-torn corner of the world. I learned about hyperarousal and how difficult it can be for some operatives to wean themselves off the constant adrenaline feed of active duty and reassimilate into normal society. With all that going against them, it is a tribute to the glue of love that holds military families together in the face of such a difficult vocation.

In this book I explore the damage done to a young girl by a distant and difficult military father but juxtapose that with the best qualities of militarism—integrity, honor, courage—in the man she comes to love and trust her own child with.

This story is set in one of my favorite parts of the world, Western Australia's deep southwest among towering karri trees and abundant wildlife. I hope readers all over the world will get a sense of what makes Western Australia's wilderness—and the people who live in it—so special.

I hope you enjoy watching the glue of love thickening between Romy, Clint and little Leighton in *The Soldier's Untamed Heart*.

Best,

Nikki Logan

NIKKI LOGAN
The Soldier's Untamed Heart

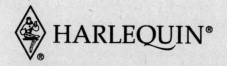

HARLEQUIN®

TORONTO • NEW YORK • LONDON
AMSTERDAM • PARIS • SYDNEY • HAMBURG
STOCKHOLM • ATHENS • TOKYO • MILAN • MADRID
PRAGUE • WARSAW • BUDAPEST • AUCKLAND

If you purchased this book without a cover you should be aware that this book is stolen property. It was reported as "unsold and destroyed" to the publisher, and neither the author nor the publisher has received any payment for this "stripped book."

Recycling programs
for this product may
not exist in your area.

ISBN-13: 978-0-373-74075-8

THE SOLDIER'S UNTAMED HEART

First North American Publication 2011

Copyright © 2010 by Nikki Logan

All rights reserved. Except for use in any review, the reproduction or utilization of this work in whole or in part in any form by any electronic, mechanical or other means, now known or hereafter invented, including xerography, photocopying and recording, or in any information storage or retrieval system, is forbidden without the written permission of the publisher, Harlequin Enterprises Limited, 225 Duncan Mill Road, Don Mills, Ontario, Canada M3B 3K9.

This is a work of fiction. Names, characters, places and incidents are either the product of the author's imagination or are used fictitiously, and any resemblance to actual persons, living or dead, business establishments, events or locales is entirely coincidental.

This edition published by arrangement with Harlequin Books S.A.

For questions and comments about the quality of this book please contact us at Customer_eCare@Harlequin.ca.

® and TM are trademarks of the publisher. Trademarks indicated with ® are registered in the United States Patent and Trademark Office, the Canadian Trade Marks Office and in other countries.

www.eHarlequin.com

Printed in U.S.A.

Nikki Logan lives next to a string of protected wetlands in Western Australia, with her long-suffering partner and a menagerie of furred, feathered and scaly mates. She studied film and theater at university, and worked for years in advertising and film distribution before finally settling down in the wildlife industry. Her romance with nature goes way back, and she considers her life charmed, given she works with wildlife by day and writes fiction by night—the perfect way to combine her two loves. Nikki believes that the passion and risk of falling in love are perfectly mirrored in the danger and beauty of wild places. Every romance she writes contains an element of nature, and if readers catch a waft of rich earth or the spray of wild ocean between the pages she knows her job is done.

Visit Nikki at her website, www.nikkilogan.com.au.

For Maus

Kristi, you endured the worst year of your life while I was enjoying the best of mine. Romy is someone I'd like to have in my corner in a difficult time, I hope I was there for you in yours. Thank you for lending me your boys.

I want to acknowledge the assistance of Squadron Leader Jeff Newton of the Royal Australian Air Force (who has some of the strongest glue I've ever seen going on in his family) and Ammon Hontz (ret. U.S. Army) for their military insight and assistance.

To Sandra and Kate, my walking buddies and beta-readers, there's a little bit of each of you in this one, girls. Thanks for being a fantastic cheer squad.

CHAPTER ONE

IT WAS hard to know what was putting the *doof-doof* into Romy Carvell's heartbeat—the illicit thrill of slipping a fine crystal ornament unseen into her coat pocket, or the lean, mean, gorgeous machine squatted chatting to her son two aisles away. She glanced surreptitiously in the convex mirror mounted over the counter. It was supposed to help them monitor the park gift shop but, right now, it conveniently gave her a perfect tool to watch anyone watching her.

The ornament clanked gently against the two other items she'd stolen as it nestled into the deep recesses of her light coat.

Her gaze drifted back to the crouched man talking to Leighton. Her son was listening but not responding, par for the course lately. Silence or conflict. Something about being eight years old. The fact he hadn't yet made a beeline for her side meant he was feeling comfortable about the stranger's presence, which instantly made Romy feel comfortable about it. The man straightened and reached for something on a nearby shelf.

Her gut twisted.

Military.

Forget the due-for-a-cut hair, the three-day growth—military didn't just wash off. This stranger had the residual carriage, the unmistakable forced casualness disguising a well-honed subliminal alertness.

He moved just like her father.

The man smiled at her son and then stepped away, giving him the space he needed. Leighton relaxed further now his escape route to his mum wasn't closed off by a human roadblock, his gentle grey eyes searching her out.

And right on their tail was this stranger's piercing green ones; they locked on Romy in the security mirror. She looked away, her heart thumping.

Okay... Definitely the man and not the shoplifting.

She shifted out of the mirror's range and pulled her focus back to the job at hand, fanning herself with the tourism postcard she'd plucked from the overcrowded carousel stand. A lot rode on her success this morning and she was taking a big risk going for one more. Not because of the oblivious cashier whose attention was locked firmly on Mr Military over there—that only made her task all the easier. But those too-casual jade eyes monitoring her every move... *They* were the most likely danger to her chances of walking out of here with what she needed.

Romy drifted across his line of sight, feeling his focus glued on her even though his outward attention had returned to Leighton. Another military trait.

Just one more. Something spectacular. Something to really drive her message home. She picked up item after item and replaced them with care, moving casually towards the glass cabinet holding an array of opal and gold jewellery that probably sold like hot cakes to the wealthy tourists that frequented WildSprings Wilderness Retreat. The display was stupidly positioned, perfect for catching customer attention but in the worst possible spot for surveillance by the single cashier. And the mirror didn't quite throw this far.

Which suited her fine.

With the efficiency of someone who had nothing at all to lose, she slid open the concealed base to the cabinet and picked out the most expensive-looking clunker she could find. Hardly the sort of thing she'd ever wear—her own tastes ran to something a little finer, something a lot cheaper—but she wasn't going to have it long. She tucked the gaudy brooch deep into her inside pocket and slid the drawer silently closed.

'Are you planning on paying for that?'

Romy was too well trained to flinch at the deep, cool voice, no matter how much her body itched to. She turned slowly, then tilted her gaze to his. *Whoa.* She'd thought he was a giant before...

He had to be six foot three, maybe four, and was built like the tank she was sure he would have travelled in once. All hard angles and iron. Her stomach dropped, but she plastered on an intentionally vague expression. 'I'm sorry?'

'Will you be buying that or just keeping the flies

off with it?' He nodded to the postcard in her hand, the one still automatically fanning her face. Her skin bristled. His tone was casual but she recognised the steel behind the smile all too well.

She'd grown up a human metal detector.

She started to move away, eager to escape the whirlpool surrounding his eyes. 'It's warmer than I expected, today.'

'Could have something to do with your coat,' he said lightly, following her. 'Wrong sort of day for a long jacket.'

Oh, Lord, she was sprung.

Her heart hammered. If he'd had anything solid on her he would have asked her to turn out her pockets by now, but he was definitely sniffing. She frowned. What was he, security? No, she was interviewing for the position of park security officer in about forty minutes, so who was this guy, some kind of good Samaritan?

She straightened to give herself one more pointless inch against him. 'Planning ahead. I heard the weather here on the south coast can be unpredictable.'

Those intense eyes weren't fooled. They scanned her down and up again as though he had X-ray vision, and when they returned to hers they were arctic.

Time to go.

She turned her face a fraction but didn't take her focus from the man in front of her. She couldn't if she'd wanted to. 'Leighton, honey. Let's go.'

Three feet of dark curls and sunshine bounded over to where Romy stood dwarfed by the stranger. He held out a card with tiny, four-toed footprints printed on it, his voice hushed. 'Mum, look. Frog prints.'

She dragged her attention down to her son and squatted. It was her personal rule. Leighton rarely sought attention these days, so when he did she gave it unquestioningly. So different to her own upbringing.

She tried to ignore the intense stare pounding onto her like a waterfall. 'Are they real?'

'Yeah. The frogs walked on the ink first, then the card. Non-toxic,' he said importantly, 'on account of the frog's sensitive skin, Clint says.'

Romy's hand faltered as it stroked her son's shoulder. She bit the inside of her cheek. *Clint?* Lord, even the name was sexy. And somehow he'd gotten more out of her son in two minutes than she had all day.

She flipped the card over and looked at the price tag. Inflated, but not completely out of the question, particularly if she could nail this job interview. She straightened. 'Tell you what, L, why don't you take your frog print and my postcard to the lady at the counter and we'll head out.'

'Is it time for your meeting?'

Romy winced. She didn't want Mr Military knowing her business. She handed her son the postcard and twenty dollars. 'Go ahead, honey. I'll be right there.'

The moment Leighton was outside hearing range, Clint spoke, suspicion narrowing his eyes even further. 'You have an appointment?'

Not that it's any of your business. 'Yes, and I need to be—'

'What kind of appointment?'

Every part of her tightened like a slingshot. *Oh, you really don't want to push that button, mister.* She'd spent a lifetime being cut off by an overbearing bully. She didn't need it today of all days. She took a shaky breath.

'I've interrupted your shopping,' she said, all courtesy. Verbal Judo 101. 'And I must be going. Excuse me.'

She was sure it was no accident he'd positioned himself between her and the exit. She squeezed past his bulk in the narrow aisle, tucking her coat to the side so the objects hidden within didn't clank against him. As she passed, she caught a whiff of something divine. Sandalwood, earth and…man. He might look as though he lived on the streets but he smelled heavenly. And all that bulk was hard as a rock, too, as she slid past him towards the counter, willing her heartbeat to settle.

So he hadn't let himself go, entirely.

'Perhaps I'll see you around?' He had the chest for such a cavernous voice. His words easily found her ears even though she'd moved halfway across the room. In her periphery, she saw him drift to the rear of the store and continue his browsing.

Lord, I hope not.

'Is that all?' the cashier politely asked.

Romy smiled at the girl, her heart beating loud enough to hear, conscious of the four stolen items hidden in her pockets and that the innocent cashier was likely to wear the temporary blame for their loss.

The angels will forgive me, she told herself.

It's necessary.

'You want to take the interviews?' Justin Long stared at his brother, bemused. With good reason. Clint knew he hadn't involved himself in the running of WildSprings for months. Years.

'Not all of them, Justin. Only this last one.' He tapped the lone female name on the list for the park security vacancy. It had to be her. The irony was perfect; he couldn't pin it, but the dark-haired beauty in the gift shop was up to something. She was too tense roaming those aisles. How many women got uptight shopping?

Justin's assistant stared at Clint as if he'd just hauled himself out of a sewer. Technically speaking, Simone was *his* assistant but she'd only ever worked with his brother so Clint forgave her confusion. It wasn't her fault he'd appeared out of nowhere, after all this time, looking like a feral animal.

He stared right back. Simone nearly stumbled in her haste to pick up something to do. Clint turned back to Justin.

'What time is this guy coming in?' He tapped the second to last name on the list.

'He's not, he withdrew this morning.'

'Can we bump Ms Carvell up?'

'I'm not even sure if she's—'

'She's here. Let's bring her over in ten minutes.' He'd rather see her right now, throw her off her game, but he needed the time to sharpen up or Simone wouldn't be the only one thinking he'd stumbled in off the streets.

Justin glared at him. 'Where am I supposed to go while you use my office?'

'Where did you used to go before you *had* an office?' He deserved the filthy look Justin threw him; he didn't play the big-brother card very often, the boss card even less. But he wasn't moving on this one.

Eight minutes and a field shave later, Clint stretched back in Justin's chair and flipped open Romy Carvell's file. His eyes flicked unconsciously to her marriage status. She was a single mother. And trying out for a security coordinator role, despite her youth.

Interesting.

The assistant's voice interrupted him. 'Ms Carvell to see you, Mr, uh, sir.'

Clint snapped the file shut and pulled himself to his feet in an automatic at-ease. Romy Carvell may be up to no good but she was still a female and, in his world, a man stood for a woman. Romy smiled politely at Simone and passed her in the doorway, then stopped in her tracks when she saw who waited for her in the office.

You? She didn't speak but her body said it for her.

'Welcome to WildSprings officially, Ms Carvell. I'm Clint McLeish.'

She recovered her composure in seconds, sliding

calmly into the vacant seat opposite his and pinning him with those amazing eyes. Battle-ash grey.

'Do you always scope out potential staff before interviews?' she asked, referring to their earlier encounter.

'Purely opportunistic.' He sank into Justin's chair and studied the woman in front of him. Nervous, but hiding it. She wanted this job badly enough not to turn and walk out when she realised she was set up. Maybe she needed it? Clint thought about the young boy in the gift shop.

'How old are you?' He blurted it out before thinking.

Her lips thinned. 'My résumé doesn't include that for a reason, Mr McLeish.'

'You think you'll be judged by your age?'

'You're judging me now. Wondering how someone my age accrued the experience I have.'

Her darkened eyes flashed and his body matched it, deep inside. The angry flush did amazing things to her bone structure. 'Actually, I was contemplating how you could possibly have a son Leighton's age. You must have been virtually a child yourself?'

She gasped and shot to her feet. Clint knew he deserved the outraged expression on her face. Man, he really had been away from people too long. He stood as well.

'Please, sit, Ms Carvell. I apologise, that was unnecessary.' He sank back into the chair as she reluctantly did, too. 'The point I'm trying to make—rather badly—is you appear very young for someone in the security industry.'

He did the math; she had to be no more than twenty-six.

She glared for a moment. 'I learned a long time ago to turn my appearance to my advantage,' she said. 'It often gives me an edge over others. They underestimate me.'

I'll bet they do. He looked at those doe eyes set in smooth skin over knockout bone structure. The mouth, which would be full if it wasn't pulled tight with displeasure. *Focus, McLeish.* He forced his mind onto the task at hand, ignoring the daggers Little Miss Fierce stared at him.

'Uh, can you give me a recent example, please?' It was textbook interview protocol and he loathed that it was coming out of his mouth. But this wouldn't be the first time he'd done something he hated based on a hunch.

She regarded him for a moment, seemed to weigh something in her mind and then reached to unbutton her coat. 'I can give you a very recent example.'

Idiot, you didn't ask for her coat. He mentally shook his head. Maybe his Grizzly Adams days were catching up with him.

Bottomless grey steel looked hard at him. 'Why were you watching me in the gift shop?'

There was no good answer to that question, so he went for a half-truth. 'You looked shifty.'

Her lips quirked, taking all the ice out of those eyes,

turning them from storm-grey to kitten-grey in a blink. 'Shifty? How?'

'Like you were up to no good.'

'I *was* up to no good. I was stealing you blind.' She reached into her pockets and pulled out an array of items he recognised. Stock from his shop. When she placed a clunky brooch on the desk, he knew exactly when she'd nabbed it. And under whose nose. Heat flared up his throat.

Bloody hell. He'd just been scammed by a rookie.

'You stopped me on instinct,' she said. 'Why didn't you take it further?'

Because I was too busy wondering what was beneath that coat of yours, and not of the stolen variety. He glared at her and realised with some pain exactly how far the mighty had fallen. He used to specialise in hostage extraction on foreign soil, now he couldn't even spot a shoplifter at six paces. He fought the stiffening of his body, knowing she wouldn't miss it. Not wanting to give her the satisfaction. 'Point taken, Ms Carvell.'

'This is hideous, by the way.' She pointed to the brooch. 'Why do you stock it?'

He had no idea; someone else did the stock selection for him. Yet another thing he'd relinquished control of since coming home. 'Because it sells?'

She shook her dark auburn hair, just like her son's but heavier and longer, and when she smiled a tiny dimple formed on her left cheek. 'It's still a crime against taste.'

Clint's brows shot up. When was the last time some-one had spoken to him with frankness and honesty rather than fear and suspicion? Or pity? *God, it felt good!*

'Stealing from me was a risk, Ms Carvell. What if I'd thrown you out?'

'A calculated risk. And I figure if you're recruiting for security you wouldn't have anyone to throw me out.'

That dimple again. Ouch. 'You doubt I could manage that on my own?' He had at least twelve inches and one hundred pounds on her.

'I figured you wouldn't have chosen to interview me yourself only to throw me out.' She nodded at his surprise. 'I did my research. I was supposed to be meeting a Mr Long.'

His reassessment was immediate. She may look as though she'd just left college but she'd worked a string of good security positions; she read people well, was thorough with research and had raised a young boy alone.

And she totally had his number.

His body stirred at the challenge. 'What would you do differently in the shop?' he asked, trying to force the interview, and his mind, back on mission.

She shrugged out of her coat and twisted to drape it over the back of the seat. Her short blouse bunched sideways and, for a fleeting moment, it lifted to expose a stretch of smooth, pale lower back marked by black ink. Clint's gaze fell on the stylised wedge-tailed eagle tattooed at the base of her spine. Its wings spanned the breadth of her hips and its majestic head disappeared behind the hem of her plain blouse.

He dragged his stare up to her face as she turned, his heart beating painfully. Only a handful of people knew his squad call sign was 'Wedgetail.' What were the chances of a civilian turning up with one tattooed so prominently on her body?

Pretty damn small.

The old feelings came surging in, the mistrust and the doubt. He fought them off with reason. How many espionage-trained operatives brought along eight-year-old accomplices? Then again, how many looked like the woman in front of him?

Only the good ones. He took a series of deep breaths and tuned in to her animated answer.

'...and you might consider moving the counter, too. It's perfectly positioned to watch the door but terrible for watching the whole store. Deter, detect, delay.' Her entire demeanour changed when she was problem solving. That brightness in her eyes, the way she leaned forwards slightly, the tilt of her head to the left as she was reasoning. She rattled on for another sixty seconds. She certainly didn't seem to have an agenda, other than showing him how crap WildSprings's security had become while he wasn't on point.

She reined in her galloping enthusiasm long enough to note his expression. 'What?'

'You noticed all of this in the few minutes you were

in the store?' Clint asked her. She shrugged. 'Tell me why I should hire you, Ms Carvell.'

She measured him with her eyes. 'I have immediate experience in a wildlife setting and I specialise in perimeter control. A park this size is going to be difficult to manage if you can't secure your boundaries. I've also worked on retail security and I have outstanding networks in state enforcement, customs and—'

He thrust up a hand. 'Plenty of people have the background for this job. Tell me why I should hire *you*.'

One perfectly shaped brow rose as he cut her off and she took a deep breath. 'Because I'm hungry for the job. I don't come with baggage or an agenda or some kind of burning desire to run the place. I enjoy what I do and I thrive on challenge but you won't lose me the moment I get comfortable in the job. I'm loyal and I'm honest…'

He tried not to glance at the array of stolen items on the desktop.

'…and I'm very good at what I do,' she finished up, sitting high in her chair, leaning towards him intently. It would be so easy to trust those steady eyes. Except trust was a stranger around here.

'You haven't been very honest today,' he said.

'Neither have you.'

Clint sat back. She had a point. 'So what aren't you good at? What are your weaknesses?' Anxiety flared and faded in those grey eyes in a heartbeat. But not so fast he didn't see it.

'I'm not brilliant at adhering to routine. It isn't in my nature. I realise that might be a sticking point given your...' She faltered. 'Given where you're from.'

Mental sirens started wailing. She'd looked into his past? His voice was dangerously cool as he asked her, 'And where's that?'

She cleared her throat. 'Your military background.'

Only a dozen civilians knew he was a Taipan. Every hair on his body stood erect. He leaned forwards, his voice subzero. 'What military background?'

She stared him down. 'Every inch of you is military. Special Forces, I'm guessing, by the way you like to intimidate people. I understand if you prefer not to discuss it but please do me the courtesy of not treating me like an idiot.'

He reined in his heartbeat and sheer willpower forced the tension out of his body. 'You don't look intimidated.'

She straightened until he thought she might snap. 'I grew out of the habit. It takes a lot more than arrogance to get under my skin these days, Mr McLeish.'

Thoughts tumbled through his mind in quick succession. First, that he'd really like to discover what *did* get under her skin. Second, it had to be her ex who'd been in the military; he'd never got a clearer anti-forces vibe from anyone. Third, she was the first person to call him arrogant to his face without even blinking. And, most pressing, that he really wanted to hear his name on her lips.

Justin was going to be so pissed.

'Call me Clint, Ms Carvell. Since we're going to be working together.'

She watched him, warily. 'You're hiring me?'

The harder she tried to mask her excitement the more colour stained her cheeks. He wondered if she'd intentionally hit every one of his weak points. The kid. The eyes. The virginal blush.

'It takes guts to pull off what you did today, and also a keen understanding of operational vulnerabilities. That tells me you know your stuff and you're prepared to take risks.'

Her body language changed in a flash and the colour drained out of her. 'I can't afford to take risks, Mr McLeish. I have a son to think about. If this job represents any kind of danger, then I'll have to pass.'

'Clint. And there is no danger—it was a figure of speech. But young boys will always find trouble if they're looking for it. We have electric fences, deep stretches of bush between our luxury chalets.' He paused and swallowed hard. 'Dams. A wilderness property still has plenty of potential danger.'

She watched him warily. 'No more than the city, I imagine. But it offers one thing the city can't for an eight-year-old nature freak. Wildlife. Leighton will die when he hears we get to stay.'

She's doing this for her son. The realisation hit him like a mortar. For all her extremely convincing claims to be seeking challenge, a role to get her teeth into, she was really looking for a safe place to bring up her son.

A sanctuary.

He was hardly in a position to judge since he'd come to WildSprings for precisely the same reason….

'Are you aware accommodation is part of the deal?' he asked. If young Leighton wanted wildlife he wouldn't be disappointed. The mile between his house and theirs was packed with all manner of creatures. One mile. The closest anyone had come to being a neighbour in…forever. Three years at WildSprings and eleven years in the Defence Force before that. No fixed address. What the hell was he going to do with a neighbour? Apart from the obvious…

Avoid them.

'I wasn't, no. But it makes sense to have security on-site this far from town.'

'Can't imagine yourself in all this tranquillity?'

'On the contrary.' Her stare bored into him. 'I look forward to the solitary existence very much.'

He straightened. Message sent and received.

Well, that was fine with him. He had no interest in playing happy neighbours no matter who her son reminded him of. The more space Romy Carvell gave him, the happier he'd be regardless of whatever this was arcing between them. There was no chance she'd let him close enough to form any kind of friendship and he had no interest in one.

Plus, he was now her boss, which put a really fat bullet in any possible chance of anything ever starting up between them. Not that she'd be seeing him again; in precisely twelve minutes he'd be returning to the privacy of his forest cabin, his massive DVD collection, his rapidly expanding library and his blessed MIA status.

Little Miss Snarky was now officially his brother's problem. He looked at all five foot three of bristling hostility putting her coat on and grinned.

Oh, Justin was going to be *so* pissed.

CHAPTER TWO

'LOST something?'

Romy popped her head from behind the latest box to see Clint McLeish filling her new doorway. She winced, knowing how filthy she was. She'd peeled off her cotton shirt hours ago as the afternoon had warmed, and her tank top, shorts and tennis shoes were all smudged with a day full of house moving. Her hair sprang wildly about her face, what strands of it weren't stuck to the sweat on her forehead.

Great.

Still, he was her boss. It was a good thing if he saw she was a hard worker. She glanced around. 'Nope, just unpacking. I haven't had a chance to lose anything yet.'

'I meant this.' He stood aside and Leighton squeezed past him into the house.

'Hey, Mum,' her boy chirped like a magpie as he disappeared up the stairs to his bedroom, dumping his backpack along the way. 'Clint is our neighbour!'

Romy closed her eyes and groaned inwardly. Letting her minidynamo out to expend all his boyish excitement outdoors had not included popping around to visit the neighbours. She held the screen door open for Clint to enter. 'Please tell me he didn't turn up at your house?'

'Not quite, but he was close.'

'I asked him to stay on the track.' She hated the defensive tone in her voice but knew she'd let more time pass than she realised. Great first impression. *Security coordinator loses own son.*

His smile was thin. 'He did, but not on your track.'

She suddenly realised where the fork about half a mile back must lead. Her mumbled apology was entirely inadequate. The man reeked of solitude and her eight-year-old cyclone had just barged into his serenity.

'Can I offer you something to drink? Beer?'

'Thanks, no,' he said coldly. 'I don't mean to intrude. I wanted to get your boy back to you safely. You must have been worried.'

'Yes…' *If I wasn't the worst mother in the world.* Courtesy demanded she should persist. 'I'm dying for a break myself. Coffee, then?'

His lips pressed together. 'Sure, thank you.' He glanced around cautiously and cleared a stray box from the dining table so he could sit. 'I saw the moving van leave just after breakfast. You've done all this today?'

He didn't look all that pleased to be staying, it had to be said. Romy set the kettle on to boil and followed his gaze into the living area where most of the boxes were now folded flat and stacked for storage by the stairs. A few pictures lined the walls and her lavender throws draped casually on the sofas.

'I specialise in unpacking.'

His eyes narrowed to slits. 'You move around a lot?'

Romy swallowed, cursing herself for opening that particular door. 'Not any more. I wanted to get us settled in so Leighton can wake up to a fully furnished house.' She'd have to work late into the night to pull it off, but since her dance card was conveniently blank...

Moving house at all went against everything she'd ever wanted for her child. Uprooting him from school, dragging him three hundred kilometres away into the forest. But the chance to get him away from the rotten neighbourhood they lived in—and his grandfather— had been too good to resist. Even if it brought back uncomfortable memories of being dragged from base to base.

'Did you find the air con?' Clint's sceptical glance at her appearance made the question redundant.

They had air conditioning? That would have been good to know two hours ago. Romy stretched her sweaty back and ran a self-conscious hand through the damp thickness of her hair. 'I wasn't really warm enough to go looking.' *Liar.* 'Where's the controller?'

He pulled his considerable bulk out of her dining chair and crossed to a small door beneath the stairs, the storage area she'd earmarked for all her packing boxes. He opened it and bent to reach inside, then emerged with a cream remote in his hand.

'I installed it in here to keep it out of sight.'

'*You* put the air-con system in?' He didn't strike her as the handy sort.

Most likely to survive on a deserted island with three beans and a paperclip... Without doubt.

He pointed the remote at a tiny red LED in the ceiling that Romy thought was a fire sensor and pressed it. Magically, a gentle hum resonated through the entire house and icy air wafted out of subtle vents to cool her damp skin.

'Awesome! Air con!' Leighton's delighted cry drifted down from upstairs.

'Thank you. I have a feeling that's going to save us when summer fully hits.' She took the remote he passed her and returned it to its hiding place under the stairs, bending forwards into the cupboard and peering around in the dim light for the cradle.

'It's on the facing wall.' Deep male tones suddenly sounded right over her shoulder.

Romy backed out to look at the panel mounted by the door and accidentally knocked against a pair of tree trunks. Clint's legs. His hands caught her hips to stop her reversing any further into him and a live current gnawed along her skin from where his warm hands rested. She choked an apology and then studied the air-con controls intently to give her scorching cheeks time to settle.

Another great moment in first impressions. Backing, butt-first, into your boss's thighs.

She didn't need sexual experience to know how bad it must have looked from his perspective. There was a new shadow in his expression. Her stomach dropped. Maybe he'd seen her tattoo… She tugged her tank top down and swallowed hard against her gut reaction to his unspoken criticism.

The kettle singing out gave her the perfect escape. She crossed into the kitchen and poured them both a coffee, her mind racing for something diverting to say. Inspiration completely failed her.

Clint finally ended the silence himself. 'Do you need a hand shifting anything? Mattresses? Large furniture?' The offer seemed genuine but he sounded annoyed that he was making it. Like his lips were working against his will.

Romy glanced around the remaining boxes and her search fell on Leighton's three vivariums. His posse of pet tree frogs currently hung out in a temporary transport tank but she knew he'd love to get them into their regular accommodations. Seeing the five frogs settled was the fastest way to get Leighton settled, and hefting sixty kilos of glass up two flights of stairs single-handed was not high on her list of activities to look forward to.

Practicality won out over pride. 'If you could help me upstairs with L's frog tanks I'd really appreciate it.'

'He keeps frogs?' Clint took a big swallow of coffee, then moved towards the tanks to check them out.

'Since he was about six.' She still got the feeling he was helping her out against his better judgement. If they weren't so awkward and the stairs not so steep she would have told him not to bother.

Bulging biceps or not.

'That's pretty specialist. For a kid,' he said.

'He's pretty special...for a kid.' She wiped her damp hands on her shorts. The air con was doing its job but having Clint in her house was making her plain nervous. This stilted conversation wasn't helping any.

They bumped and heaved and lurched the first tank up the stairs like poorly partnered dancers until, finally, they crossed the threshold into Leighton's A-frame attic bedroom. They placed the tank down gently.

The room was ideal for a young boy with a wild imagination. A single large window looked out over a tree-packed gully behind the house like a living landscape painting, and there was plenty of ceiling space between the rafters for posters and an entire wall free for the vivariums to hold Leighton's five best friends in the world.

Lucky Leighton wasn't quite tall enough yet to bang his head on the low end of the A-frame rafters. Romy vaguely recalled the man who'd fathered him was of average height himself—average in every way, in fact—which was why she couldn't remember much about him nine years after the solitary night that had changed her life forever. If he'd been a behemoth like Clint McLeish, chances were Leighton would be rubbing a bump on his forehead right now.

She hauled in a breath.

His eyes flicked over the sci-fi models, reptile posters and mountain of books waiting for a yet-to-be-assembled bookshelf and turned to her. 'You've done well in here. It looks…'

Again with the reluctance? If he didn't want to speak to her why did he keep starting conversations?

'…different to when it was my room.'

Leighton's bright face snapped to his. 'This was your room? Cool!'

He dropped to his haunches. 'I grew up in this attic. Then I lived in the cottage for the past two years while I built my house on the other side of the valley. After I got back from the—' he seemed to catch himself '—overseas. I always preferred the view from this room.'

The enticing flash of Clint stretched out under the A-frame roof on a hot summer's evening draped in nothing but moonlight immediately put Romy in a bad mood. And he'd built his own house, too…

How very GI Joe.

'Sorry?' The glint in his eyes told her maybe she'd said it aloud.

She squared her shoulders. 'We should get the next tank in.'

His glare almost certainly matched her own as they trundled downstairs for the second trip. There was no doubt she'd ticked him off by pointing out all the security failings in his expensive wilderness retreat, but fortunately he seemed to have put the needs of his business ahead of his colossal personal ego in agreeing to hire her. Another military flow-on, she'd bet. Corps before self, every time.

In fact, it was corps before pretty much everything, including family. Wives, girlfriends…and sad, lonely little daughters.

In the living room, he waved her help away, lifted the second tank solo and mastered it up the staircase with a great deal more ease than when the two of them had failed to coordinate their efforts. Romy followed with an aluminium tank stand in each hand, doing her best to ignore the way his muscles shifted under his T-shirt and the power in the arms that spanned the metre-long tank.

Eventually all three tanks were in place and even GI Joe was puffing slightly from the effort. She tried to visualise how she might have accomplished the same on her own. It would have involved hours of straining and a good deal of swearing. Clint did it in less than five minutes. The affront to her feminine pride and the way her traitorous body was responding to the phero-mones he was pumping out in his sweat only dirtied her mood further. She plucked her tank top away from her damp skin and forced the tingles to heel.

'Thank you for your assistance,' she said as soon as they returned downstairs. 'I shouldn't keep you any longer. I'm sure you had things to do today.' She swung the screen door wide.

Not subtle.

Clint's regard was steady and he settled comfortably against the doorframe. 'Nothing I can't do tomorrow.'

Ten minutes ago he didn't want to be here. Now he wanted to move in. Romy took a deep breath and brought out the big guns. 'I've nearly finished in the living room. My bedroom's next. Unless you were really eager to unpack boxes of lingerie…?'

He didn't exactly bolt out of the door but her words had the desired effect. He peeled himself slowly off the doorframe and dug long fingers into his front pocket to retrieve his car keys. She glanced out of the window and saw a beat-up old utility sitting way back in her driveway. As if he'd tried not to disturb her by parking any closer.

He didn't need a vehicle to be disturbing. Just having him in the house had thrown her composure. She hadn't wanted to taint another household with military presence.

Too late.

She looked up at him. 'I want to say, "See you at work," but somehow I don't think I will.'

He shook his head. 'I usually don't get overly involved in the operations of WildSprings. I have staff for that.'

The less-than-subtle reminder *she* was one of his staff didn't escape her. Romy straightened on the verandah of the house and stood back, her voice cool. 'Thanks for your help today, Mr McLeish. I appreciate it.'

At the foot of the stairs, Clint watched her brows

come together in a delicate frown. So, they were back to Mr McLeish and Ms Carvell. She was yet to say his name. He turned towards his ute.

It was probably his fault. He was uncomfortable entering her house to start with, but when his hands rested on her hips as she reversed out of the stair cupboard into him, they'd been almost exactly the same span as the wings of the raptor tattooed over her spine. Two sides of him had slammed together like Norse gods—the damaged, suspicious part that took it as some kind of cosmic reminder not to get too close, and the ravenous, ex-soldier part that thought the ink art was just about the sexiest thing he'd seen in three years and wanted to feel where it branded her skin. By the time he'd marshalled his emotions she was shooting daggers at him with those extraordinary eyes.

The woman might be surveillance professional but she was lousy at hiding her thoughts. He was trained to read people—his life had depended on it for years—but Romy Carvell was a particularly open book.

And right now the book had fallen open on page 'get the hell out of here.'

Seeing young Leighton jogging along his track had been a kick in the guts, reminding him too much of another running boy, another time, and his protective instincts had come roaring to the fore. It was an elusive taste of something he'd accepted he was never going to experience. But dropping him home had been about more than taking a rare opportunity to feel like a father for five seconds. It was a chance to see Romy Carvell in her natural habitat.

He started the ute. Out of nowhere, he got the urge not to retreat to his treetop hideaway, where his books, his music, his forest awaited. He hadn't so much as looked in on park operations in ten months and he hated the thought that Romy would be judging him by the standards she found there when she started work first thing Monday morning.

He opened his window when he was side on to her, and raised his hand in a reluctant farewell. 'See you Monday, Romy.'

She plastered her hands to her hips and called after him. 'I thought you didn't get involved in operations?'

He wondered if she knew how sexy she looked standing slung like that on the verandah of his old family home. Possibly not or she wouldn't be wasting it on him. She'd made it perfectly clear how little she thought of the military and, by association, *him*. It wasn't really too different to how he felt. He pushed his sunglasses onto the bridge of his nose and looked back out at her.

'Usually,' he called out, and then accelerated out the driveway.

She shrank in his rear-vision mirror until he turned the bend. When he hit the branch-off for home he kept driving. He had the rest of Saturday night and all of Sunday to play catch-up on what had been happening at WildSprings while he was AWOL from the business side of things.

Come Monday morning he wanted to have a full handle on his business.

It was probably overdue and only had a bit to do with the auburn-haired beauty now living in his parents' cottage.

Probably.

CHAPTER THREE

THE gift shop wasn't the only part of the wilderness retreat in Romy's sights during her first week. People were obliging on her first days since a pretty young thing from the city was novelty enough without her walking around with an impressive high-tech satellite phone/GPS combo, a dark blue uniform reminiscent of the police force and taking notes wherever she went.

By day four, her new colleagues were wearying of her tight focus on their operations and her recommendations for change to improve security, but they found it easier simply to comply.

It wasn't all wins. Justin refused point-blank to consider CCTV equipment for the admissions area, arguing that some of their guests appreciated the low-key and confidential approach WildSprings offered. And the local farmer Romy busted helping himself to avocados from one of the park's many orchards voiced his outrage all round the district of having to supplement his pigs' expensive tastes out of his own pocket. It was hardly drug busts and high-tech stakeouts but it was enormously satisfying nonetheless, because it was hers.

New job, new home, new start.

Today's drama wasn't too difficult. One of her random perimeter-fence checks had turned up a breach right at the back of the park near a series of deep, crystalline dams. No doubt locals sneaking in to snare the succulent crustaceans living on the dam floor, or kids cooling off in the cold, clean depths. Except kids wouldn't have vehicles and there were definite tyre tracks coming in off a disused access road.

'Hey, Simone,' Romy greeted the admin assistant as she walked into Justin's office a few doors down from the broom closet she called her own. 'I'm heading out to do fence repair and I'll be taking the last roll of straining wire. Would you mind restocking from Garretson's?'

Simone glared up from her to-do pile and mumbled, 'Sure. What's one more boss giving me tasks?'

She kept her voice even. 'Everything okay, Simone?'

'No.' The redhead glared at her, then puffed air through her cheeks, sighing. 'It's not your fault. I know you have a job to do. It's just that my workload has trebled this week what with yourself starting and Mr McLeish suddenly reappearing.' She gestured to the work stacked on her desk.

Ah. Territory issues. 'You look like a woman who could use a coffee break.' She smiled. 'Come on. I'll fix you one.'

Simone grumbled as she emerged from behind the stack of files but followed willingly enough to the kitchenette. 'I kid you not, Romy. I hadn't seen Mr McLeish for a year before the day you came in for your interview. Then Monday morning I come in to a two-page to-do list.'

Romy poured two coffees. 'A year? Seriously?'

Simone scooted up onto the kitchenette benchtop. 'You wouldn't know, because you're new,' she started in a conspiratorial tone, 'but Clint McLeish is kind of a mystery man around here. No-one but Justin sees much of him at all.'

The last part she could believe. The man's manner practically screamed, *Leave me alone.*

'So now I have Justin and you giving me work and Mr McLeish lurking around in the shadows by day and riffling through the office overnight. It's unsettling.'

Romy's spider senses started tingling. He was working alone at night? What on?

'I get that you're new and all,' the redhead grizzled onwards, taking a healthy swallow of instant coffee, 'but we all have a first week and why he feels it's necessary to pave your way particularly, I don't know.'

Pave her way?

Simone moaned. 'Sorry. That sounds bitchy. This isn't really about you. I just wish if he was going to get so involved in someone's workload he might spare a thought for mine.' She took another swallow of coffee. 'This is like therapy—I feel heaps better for venting.'

'I don't understand,' Romy casually dropped in, going straight into investigation mode, 'whose work is he doing?'

Simone blinked at her. 'Yours. At least, some of it.'

'What?'

'He's coming in at night, Romy. Working on park security. I thought you knew?'

'How would I know?'

'We assumed it was something you did. You know, in the city.'

'Even in the city I'd stop short on spying on my employer,' she said. *Unless there was good reason.* 'No wonder people are keeping me at arms-length.'

Simone's face dropped as she finally realised she'd said something wrong. 'Oh. No. That's not what I meant. We're all just getting to know you...as best we can...' she finished a bit pathetically.

Romy winced. 'Have I come on a bit strong?'

'Not strong. Just...'

Pushy? Nosey? Determined? She'd been called all three in her time.

'God. Sorry.' Simone slid off the bench. 'I'm making a real mess of this. Quendanup is the country, you know? People like to get to know everything about you. And you're a bit private, that's all. People here are already sensitive to that because of Mr McLeish, so...'

Romy relaxed. This wasn't the first time she'd had

the criticism. There was one sure way to end gossip. Satisfy it. 'What would you like to know about me?'

Simone stopped in the doorway. Chewed her lip. 'I can ask?'

'Go ahead. I have nothing to hide.' *Ha!* She leaned on the counter and forced herself to relax. 'Three questions.'

Simone slid her cup into the sink and clenched her hands in front of her, thinking fast. She spun back. 'Why did you leave the city?'

Straight for the million-dollar question. There was no good answer for that one. Except the truth. 'There was…someone…I wanted to get far away from. This seemed like a sufficient distance.' Let them think she had left Leighton's father. And it would be 'them'; she had no doubt her private business would run through the park staff like a strain of gastro. 'And I didn't like some of the kids my son was hanging out with.'

Simone thought about that and then her eyes brightened. 'Question two. How do you know Mr McLeish?'

Romy tilted her head. 'What makes you think I do?'

Simone laughed. 'He emerges from his forest for the first time in a year on the day you happen to be interviewing for a job. Then he hires you, having made not one single business decision since Justin arrived. Then he helps you move house…'

How did people *know* this stuff? Were the forest possums running a blog?

'…and, finally, the pair of you have enough chemistry to start a bushfire. That doesn't evolve overnight.'

Romy shook her head. 'You saw us together for about twenty seconds after the interview, Simone.'

'I could *feel* the tension in the room. The vibe between the two of you was the closest to action I've had in a while, let me tell you.'

'The only tension you felt was irritation. He was ticked off because I embarrassed him about his store security. And he hired me for the same reason. Besides, if he hasn't emerged for that long, where am I supposed to have met him?'

'Oh, he comes out, just not amongst people here. Supposedly he heads up to the city a couple of times a year for… You know…'

She shook her head, bemused. 'For?'

Simone's mouth opened and then closed again and a blush stained her pretty features.

Romy stiffened immediately. 'Let me see if I have this right. People here think I know Clint McLeish from the city where he sometimes goes to *pick up*.'

Simone flushed to her roots. 'Um…'

'And him hiring me unexpectedly is some kind of evidence the two of us are an item? Oh, that's right, let's not forget the explosive chemistry zinging around when we're together. Can't keep our hands off each other. I suppose he's also the father of my child, yes?'

She didn't know skin could turn so crimson. Romy slammed her mug on the sink in disbelief. 'Oh, you are kidding me! For the record, Simone, my son's father is not Clint McLeish. He and I had never met. We are not secret lovers. He's not helping me do my work. And there is no chemistry—he doesn't even like me particularly. Can I be any clearer?'

Her pitch had risen considerably and her chest heaved with anger. Simone backed away a step or two during her outburst but then stood her ground, silently assessing. Romy stared at her through steady, furious eyes.

'I believe you. I'm sorry if I jumped to the wrong conclusion.'

Romy could only nod.

'I wouldn't want anyone saying something about you that's not true.' Serious blue eyes stared steadily at Romy. The irony was exquisite.

Simone chewed her lip. 'But…he *is* working on security at night—it's the only thing he's touching. I'm not mistaken about that.'

Romy's heart squeezed with familiar pain. He was doing her work for her. She'd clearly made a very bad first impression if he thought her so incapable. 'Then I'll take it up with him,' she said tightly.

Simone nodded and turned for the door. At the last moment, she put her head back in the room. 'And, Romy, the chemistry? I'm not mistaken about that either.' She shrugged gently before turning out the door. 'Sorry.'

Romy did a fantastic job of internalising her irritation that Clint was helping her out behind the scenes, taking her frustration out on the damaged fence line instead. So when she glanced down and saw his distinctive, battered ute pull up to one side of the deep, blue-green dam she was working near, she knew fate wanted her to say something.

And not just one thing.

Dumping the wire strainers and her heavy gloves onto the hard earth and tugging her broad-brim hat further down her head she marched down the slope in the direction of the dam. Flies buzzed around the perspiration on her face and throat and she shooed them away with angry flicks of her wrist, every one matching words she never, ever said in front of her son. But she said them now, and not quite under her breath.

How dared he patronise her by helping her out secretly? She was perfectly capable of doing the job she was hired for. This wasn't the first time she'd started in a new field and she had every confidence in her ability to hit the ground running. But he didn't obviously. To sneak in at night and prepare things for her, or order new equipment, or fix things before she had a chance to. It was galling!

Her furious feet moved her quickly but when she got down to the edge of the dam, Clint was nowhere to be seen. She scanned the horizon, glanced into the ute, turned and looked back the way she had come.

Silence.

'McLeish!' Her call was more of a cry to battle.

It echoed across the empty clearing before being swallowed up in the thick trees leading away from it.

Still nothing. *Damn him!*

A splash behind her had her spinning around on the spot.

'You rang?' Clint bobbed in the dam like a buoy, dunking under briefly, then emerging, glistening, and pushing his hair from his face. Wet, his features were all perfect angles and sharp, sparkling edges. Strong arms brought him closer to the shallows. 'What can I do for you, Ms Carvell?'

Romy fought to ignore the slow reveal as his feet found the dam floor. 'You can stop holding my hand,' she called out, her heart thumping.

He stopped drifting towards her and stood straighter in the water. 'Explain that to me.' His fingers came up to shield his gaze from the glare and sunlight bounced off the rivulets streaming down the hard planes of his chest.

She ignored that, too.

She swallowed to put some moisture back in her mouth. 'You're doing my job for me.' She didn't have to yell now he was only metres away from where she stood on the dam's edge. He looked so infuriatingly confident standing there like some kind of aquatic god. While she was all sweaty and revolting.

Again.

That fired her up even more. 'I'm perfectly capable of doing the job you're paying me to do. I don't need your help. I don't want it.'

'Who says I'm helping you?' His legs carried him through the shallows and the dam seemed to drop away from him as he approached.

Her breath hitched as first broad pecs and then a ridged stomach emerged from the water, then it released on a whoosh when his feet found the ascent to shore and pushed a pair of dark board shorts, slung low on angular obliques, into view.

Not that she was looking.

'You're coming in at night and doing things before I can get to them.' *Deny it,* she wanted to shout.

He dragged his feet onto the sand and stopped in front of her, dropping his arm from his eyes, suspicion live in the shadowed gaze. 'How do you know what I'm doing at night?'

Great. Another person who thought she was capable of a bit of internal espionage. But she was loath to get Simone in trouble, not after the hard time she'd already given her.

She hedged. 'Is it true or not?'

Dark lashes clumped by water droplets blinked down over vibrant green eyes. No wonder the townspeople had such a romantic view of him; between the face and the intrigue, he was mysterious and handsome enough to be flashing on feminine radars across the south-west.

Her own was going ballistic right now.

'It's true I'm working at night,' he said.

'And...?'

'And it's true I'm looking at some aspects of our

security—' Romy turned to stalk off. A strong, wet
hand wrapped around her elbow and drew her back.
'But relax. I'm not doing you any special favours. Why
would I? I hardly know you.'

Oh.

He might as well have slapped her across the face
with a wet reality fish. Romy groaned inwardly and
called herself all manners of idiot. She'd allowed her
own complexes to totally feed off Simone's skewed
view of what was going on in the office after dark.
He was right. Why *would* he help her out?

'Why do you care, anyway?' He lifted a towel from
the tray of his ute and patted his face and neck dry.
That was when she saw the tattoo, beautifully positioned on his left bicep. A sword surrounded by a gar-
land of snakes.

'Because I'm more than capable of doing any part of
this job. I don't need backup.' Before he could open his
mouth, she barrelled on. 'So whatever you're working
on it might be smart to keep me in the loop so we're
not double-handling.'

He slung the towel over his shoulder. 'It doesn't
matter—I'm nearly done, anyhow.' *Dismissed.* His
imperious tone got right up her nose. Reminded her
of another man. An older man.

'Going back into hiding for another twelve months?'
She could have bitten her tongue off the moment the
bitchy comment slipped out.

He shook his head. 'Are you always this unpleasant?' His words were as cool as the water evaporating off his skin. They just begged to be challenged.

She took a deep breath. 'I don't buy this whole brooding, damaged act, you know. I'm sure it does great things for your reputation in town but it's been a couple of years—don't you think it's getting a little old?'

His eyes narrowed to slits. 'So now you're familiar with my past and all? That's a bit like me saying your high-and-mighty act is getting tired.'

A needle stabbed through Romy's chest. High and mighty? Why that hurt particularly, after everything she'd been called in life... Yet her voice was tight when she responded.

'You'll have to do better than that, McLeish. I've had every name under the sun thrown at me and survived it. I'm resistant to sticks and stones, too. Too many calluses.'

He blinked slowly and considered her. 'By who?'

Whoa. How did they get here? She only wanted to call him on the extracurricular night-school activity. She backed off, fists clenched tight. 'I have to get on with the fence. Excuse me.'

'You were out here working?'

She pointed to the fence line silhouetted against the glare at the top of the hill and he followed her gaze sceptically. 'Relax, McLeish. I'm not stalking you. Why would I? I hardly know you.'

His own words flung back at him, he smiled. '*You* know how to string a fence?'

The doubt in his voice got her blood racing. 'You think you're the only one who gets to be capable? What is it with you military types?'

His rebuttal was soft. 'The question is, what is it with *you* and military types?'

She glared at him. '*That* is none of your beeswax.'

Good one, Romy, you sound all of twelve years old. Ignoring the amused sparkle in his eye, she tossed her hair back over her shoulder and powered on up the hill, swishing at the flies the whole way.

'Let me give you a hand with that.' Clint appeared behind her and held out a pair of gloves.

Having assured herself with a quick glance that he was fully dressed now, Romy focused on the wire in her hands. 'I don't need help, thanks.'

'I know you don't, but I'd like to…'

She squinted into the open sincerity on his face and made to thank him. Then he went and ruined it.

'…and I'm the boss, so what I say goes.'

She tightened a smile around the retort she was dying to spit and turned back to the torturous fence. She saw Clint flick a glance at her broken wire strainers on the ground and the arrangement she'd rigged up by proxy with a screwdriver twisted into the wire. Thanks to her angry yanking, the ratchet had broken at the crucial moment, leaving her to tighten four strands manually in century-plus heat. Every turn of the screwdriver pulled the wire that bit tighter but it was a hellish way to do it.

One strand had taken her twenty minutes.

'Go ahead,' she relented, standing carefully and letting him into her place.

He squatted at the fence line and spoke from under his Akubra hat, getting a feel for the wire. 'Can I ask you a question?'

Romy hesitated. Something told her it wasn't going to be about work. 'Sure...'

He twisted, once, twice, and then he retested the wire. The strength in the contoured triceps emerging from the sleeves of his T-shirt was distracting. He gave it two more twists until he was satisfied, then he levered the screwdriver free and turned to look up at her.

'Where's Leighton's father?'

She stared at him. She preferred the direct approach to Simone's whispered speculation but she wasn't entirely ready for the question, despite dreading it half her life. Every clever answer she'd ever imagined abandoned her.

'I don't know.' That was as honest as she could be.

The beat-up Akubra tilted curiously and the flash of green was disconcerting. 'Doesn't he see his son?'

'No.' Again, short but true.

'You don't want to talk about it?' He balanced on his haunches as though he could sit there all day.

Not with you. 'I'm not used to talking about it.'

'No-one's ever wanted to know? I find that hard to believe.'

Romy kicked the dust at her feet. 'Most people would think it was a rude question to actually *verbalise*.'

His hat lifted slightly with his eyebrows. Was that a blush creeping up his throat? Her mouth curved at the realisation it simply hadn't occurred to him not to ask. The hint of humanity made her more inclined to answer.

'He and I...parted ways a long time ago,' she said.

The understatement of all time. The spectre of the Colonel loomed. *Whore*. Worse.

Clint studied her, then spoke quietly. 'Does he know he has a son?'

Bang, right on the money. Instincts like that would have been wasted anywhere other than a specialist role. Commandos, maybe? Or Tactical Assault. She struggled to keep her anger in check as old hurts oozed up.

'I doubt he even knew he'd had sex,' she muttered grimly.

Those sea-green eyes flicked away for the barest of moments, then locked onto hers again. 'Right. Next topic?'

She took a deep breath. 'Yes, please.'

And just like that it was over. She'd shared her shame with someone. The absolute last someone she would have expected to be opening up to but he hadn't sneered or even judged her. There was nothing but compassion in those twin depths.

'Can I ask you a question?' she risked.

'Maybe.'

She perked up. 'What branch of the military were you in?'

'If I told you I'd have to kill you.' His laugh was only half joking.

'Seriously...'

He looked at her, his voice tighter than the wire he was straining. 'Does it matter?'

She kept her gaze steady. 'No. But I'm curious.'

'Don't be.'

A big part of her wanted to smack that hat right off his head. But she reined it in. 'Hey, I've just stripped myself naked for you. The least you could do is drop one article.'

Those powerful hands stopped working entirely and a deep chuckle followed like a distant rumble of thunder. 'You do have a gift for expression, Romy.'

Not deflected, she stared down into his broad shoulders until the silence grew tangible. He sighed and twisted up to her. 'I was an operative with Strike Force Taipan. Tactical Assault and Extraction.' His voice turned from grudging to irritated. 'Why are you smiling?'

Taipans. It fit. She could see him slipping over the edge of a Zodiac all camouflaged at midnight. 'Just revelling in the momentary pleasure of knowing everything. It happens very rarely.'

'Is that right?'

'I have an eight-year-old particularly gifted at

pointing out when I'm wrong.' *He took after his grandfather.*

He chuckled again, only this time she watched the grin spread over his face. It really transformed him, as if he wasn't striking enough already.

In a kill-you-with-a-well-placed-thumb kind of way.

'All done.' He pulled off the gloves and wiped his hands on his jeans, then returned to his usual position, towering over her. Romy realised how accustomed she'd become to gazing up at him. Despite always being short, it was possibly the only time she'd felt... fragile. The thought had her scrambling away from him, her voice breathy.

'Okay. Well, thanks. I guess I should be grateful nature endowed one of us with muscles.'

That smile again. 'There's more to life than brute strength. Besides, you virtually repaired this single-handed. I just got to swan in at the end and be the hero.'

At his own words, the light dimmed from his eyes. They clouded with something dark. He glanced towards his vehicle and then busied himself collecting the tools scattered across the ground. She joined him. When her toolkit was packed and there was no good reason to linger, she pulled her hat off and ran her fingers through sweat-dampened hair.

He hadn't met her eyes for minutes now. 'I guess I should get going. Thanks for the help....'

'You're welcome.' Still no eye contact but critically

polite. He collected up the broken strainer and turned towards his ute at the foot of the hill. Romy frowned. What had she said? Why did she even care? This man was nothing to her, only her employer.

But she did.

She sighed and turned away from him.

Clint felt the loss of her grey, almond-shaped eyes. It hadn't been hurt simmering away in those smoky depths; she was too protected for that. It was caution. Confusion. And something else, something older that didn't belong to him. But he felt like a heel, anyway.

'I'm sorry, Romy. I'm not angry at you.'

'Who are you angry at?' Her whispered reply drifted to him on the warm breeze. Anxious. The playful spark in her expression completely absent. Yet another thing he'd killed in this world. It was a reasonable question but impossible to answer. Hadn't he tried all these years to figure it out? Lord knows he'd had plenty of time. Somewhere along the line it got easier not to think about it any more.

He stared long and hard at her. 'Do you swim?'

Her confusion doubled. 'Why?'

'If you swim, don't do it in the dams around the cottage. Come here. This is the best for swimming.'

'I'd already gathered that.'

'Swim here.' Why was he obsessing on this?

She straightened. 'That sounds vaguely like an order.'

'Will that have more impact?'

'I'd prefer you to ask me.'

He shoved his hands deep into the pockets of his board shorts. 'Ah, sorry. Occupational hazard.'

'You can take the man out of the corps…'

'What do you know about the corps?'

'Unit. Corps. God. Country,' she said. 'Doesn't leave much room for being human.'

He squinted. 'You know the code?'

'I lived with the code.'

Her simple grimace was telling. He knew only too well the personal price soldiers paid for honouring that ideal. Family came in a poor fifth right behind your unit. The men who kept you alive, who had your back.

Or were supposed to.

For all those big, beautiful eyes seemed to know about loss, he doubted they knew squat about betrayal. The things he'd seen, things he'd done. The things others had done that he'd never been able to reconcile. She didn't have a clue. Romy Carvell was like a fresh set of combat camos: unsullied, crisp at the seams. The sort of thing you could slip into and feel clean, just for a moment until the sand leached in.

'I'm asking you, Romy. If you or Leighton swim, please make it here. Okay?'

She considered him long and hard. Then she shrugged. 'It's your property.'

Something deep inside him staggered with relief. 'What are you doing this evening?'

She blinked at his rapid change of direction. 'Uh… Helping Leighton with a science project.'

'Friday, then. There's something I'd like to show you on the estate.' And there was. But mostly it was an excuse to spend some more time with her, to sit close to those crisp, new khakis and think about how good it would feel to be clean again. 'Can you meet me in the afternoon?'

'Where?'

'I'll find you.'

She nodded and he turned down the hill, towards the twinkling green water he swam in daily, trying to baptise himself for a new beginning.

CHAPTER FOUR

I'll find you.

The words kept pinging around in Romy's head. It was only her favourite quote in her favourite movie of all time. Except now, whenever she heard it, she'd think of a jade-eyed, square-jawed giant instead of Daniel Day-Lewis in a loincloth.

Okay, so not the worst trade-off…

She tipped her head back and let the cool water from the showerhead tumble over her.

I'll find you. When a man like Clint McLeish promised that, you knew he wasn't kidding. He would find a polar bear in a blizzard in the Arctic Circle. He was just that kind of…doer.

Nothing quite as sexy as a capable man.

She twisted the cold-water tap off hard, warning herself away from those thoughts. There was a very hazy line between capable and overbearing and she'd lived half her life with the latter.

She glanced at her watch and gasped. Leighton's school bus would be dropping him at the gates to WildSprings in about four minutes. If his day was

anything like hers, he'd be hot, bothered and ready
for the air conditioning.

It took her two minutes to throw on some clothes
and get to the car. As she reached for the doorhandle,
a growing plume of dust through the trees caught her
eye. A blue Nissan cruised into her drive and pulled
up nearby. A rosy-cheeked, blonde gnome popped her
head out of the driver's side window and then pushed
the door open.

'Hi! You must be Leighton's mum? I'm Carolyn
Lawson, Cameron's mum.'

Cameron? Romy bent to glance in the rear of the
Nissan. Her son seemed absorbed in discussion with
a blond boy about the same age. A ratty blue heeler
with a lolling tongue was squished in there with them.
Carolyn Lawson was five foot nothing and nearly
as round as she was tall. But her smile was instant
and her confidence infectious. Romy's people metre
blinked happily in the green. She held out her hand and
accepted Carolyn's firm shake.

'I hope you don't mind me dropping Leighton home,'
she said. 'I wanted to introduce myself so you'd know
who we were when he came to stay.'

'To stay?' *Her* Leighton?

Both boys scrabbled out of the car and the blue
heeler exploded out the door to snuffle in the nearby
long grass. Carolyn scolded the dog as he christened
the verandah with a well-aimed stream of urine.

Romy looked at her son, her socially awkward,
struggles-to-make-friends son. 'Like a sleepover?'

Cameron groaned. 'Girls sleep over. Boys hang out,' he said, pointedly.

She laughed. 'My mistake. Does that make it a hang-over?'

The children frowned at each other in confusion but a cackle burst from Carolyn Lawson. 'No, that's what I'm likely to have after having two young boys in the house all night!' she said. 'Steve and I will both be home to keep things civil and you're welcome to call if you want to check in.'

Romy was unprepared for this eventuality. Her baby had never been on a sleepover and it hadn't occurred to her his very first one might be with a family she didn't know. Her uncertainty must have shown. Carolyn shoved a business card in her hands.

'This is our address and my mobile's on the reverse. Does it help to know Cameron's my fourth? And my husband is Quendanup's copper?'

Romy looked at her son, at the blind hope and trepidation in a face that was a miniversion of her own. The realisation he was expecting her to say no struck her like a snake. How often had she stared hopefully at her father like that? How often had he let her down? She dropped her voice and her focus to the little boy at her feet.

'You'd like to go to a sleepover, L?'

'Hangout, Mum!'

She took that as a yes. Hard to say what was more moving; the fact Leighton had made a *hangout* friend already or that he was trying so hard to look cool in front of him. And with a policeman in the house...

She turned to Carolyn Lawson. 'Thank you for the offer. Yes, I'm happy for—'

She got no further. Both boys started whooping it up in the driveway and an excited dog got in on the act, dashing around and barking.

It took ten minutes to get the Lawsons and their mad dog back in the Nissan and her overexcited son into the comparative cool of the house. Romy tried to imagine what kinds of things might happen at a kids' sleepover. Yet another experience missing from her childhood. She frowned. Had she never been asked to someone else's house, or had she said no so often the girls in her class simply stopped asking? It went without saying she'd never hosted one. Not only would the Colonel not have tolerated a gaggle of children in the house but she wouldn't have foisted him on them either.

'Mum. Can I take the frogs with me to Cameron's?' Leighton burst into the room.

Romy laughed. 'No. They're happy where they are. They'd hate being dragged to school. If you want Cameron to see them you can invite him here sometime.'

'Oh, cool!'

The fact it had never occurred to him to ask instantly highlighted the truth that he'd never brought a friend home in his life. Sorrow soaked through her. She added that to her list of things she was convinced she'd robbed him of. Like grandparents and the father-figure he so desperately craved. Only this one she could do something about.

'Leighton?' She fixed him a sandwich while he settled from his excitement. 'Would you feel okay about that? Bringing Cameron here?'

'Yeah! He can see my room. And I can show him Frog Swamp.' A muddy pocket at the base of the gully, teeming with life and riddled with wild frogs.

Boy heaven.

Romy's tension eased. Even now, the ghost of her father still had her doubting herself. Her parenting. She shook her head to clear it and turned to her boy.

'Okay. So let's talk science project…'

'Leighton?' Romy called into the silence and then listened.

Nothing.

Ugh. It was so not the evening for this. As if she wasn't already grumpy enough from continuously catching herself looking out for Clint. For a plume of dust approaching. Now Leighton had pulled another disappearing act after dinner, right when they were supposed to be preparing his science project for Friday science class.

Not the first time he'd done a runner. 'Eight-year-olds,' she muttered, turning to the house.

Fortunately, she had just the tool for this eventuality. Some mothers gave their kids phones to keep track of them; Romy gave hers a GPS transmitter. Not that he knew it. Telling him it was sewn into the hem of his backpack was the fastest way to ensure he never remembered to take the bag again.

She rustled in her work kit and pulled out her PDA. It was satellite phone, scanner and GPS tracker all in one. Swiss Army knife for the twenty-first century.

Please let him have it with him...

She got a reading almost immediately. It placed him within twenty metres of the kitchen. She frowned and looked at the timber ceiling above her. *Damn...*

A quick bolt to the top of the stairs confirmed her suspicion. The backpack lay tossed in the corner of his shambolic attic room. So much for technology; she was going to have to do this the old-fashioned way. Romy pocketed the PDA and let herself out the screen door to the rear of the house. She glanced one way, up the long track leading past Clint's to the park entry, and then the other way, down through the trees leading to the base of the gully.

Frog Swamp. It's where she'd be if she was an eight-year-old amphibian fanatic trying to avoid homework. And if Leighton didn't have his pack it meant he'd planned to stay close.

There wasn't a child alive who knew more about snakes than her reptile-mad son so she didn't worry on that score, but the Australian bush was full of holes to twist an ankle in, poisonous critters with fangs to sink in their self-defence and baffling thickets of trees that could swallow a young boy's sense of direction in a heartbeat.

Turning left, she started picking her way along the old trail that led to the bottom of the gully where the wetlands were. It was increasingly beautiful as the earth dropped away at the foot of towering trees stretching to the heavens. Small lizards scurried across her path and butterflies flitted kamikazelike back and forth. She slowed her descent and glanced about, appreciating the beauty of the bush around her at dusk.

As she worked her way quietly to the gully floor she heard a hint of noise off to the left. She was tempted to call out but the utter silence around her restrained her. If Leighton was frog watching he'd scarcely appreciate her dulcet tones echoing through the valley and sending every living creature darting for cover. Besides, she was being calm, cool Mum today, not anxious, clingy Mum.

That mum wouldn't kick in for at least another five minutes.

A flash of bright red caught her eye. Her shoulders sagged with relief and she started towards her son. Then suddenly a shift of blue right next to him. A sky-blue T-shirt stretched tight over a broad back. She stumbled to a halt.

Clint.

Leighton was smiling. Not a polite, adult-pleasing smile. A bright-eyed, face-splitting, genuine boy grin, as he looked back and forth from where Clint lay next to him in the dirt to the swampy soak in front of them. She stopped and watched. Neither of them spoke but they seemed to be communicating in a kind of sign language. Clint's efficient hand symbols reeked of the military but Leighton's overengineered, highly dramatic efforts did somehow manage to communicate.

Her heart gave a little lurch. They were dusk frog watching together. It was postcard perfect. Everything she'd never had with her father.

And her son would never have with his.

Leighton was laid out like a miniature version of Clint. He unconsciously mirrored the exact way the older man lay in the earth, short legs stretched out next to long ones, torso propped up onto his elbows like his adult shadow. The ultimate Hallmark moment.

Never mind that L's feet stopped a good metre higher than Clint's. It put them dead parallel with a sinfully well-packed, denim-clad rear which was why it was so easy for Romy's gaze to drift and linger there. She tore them back to her son. His wildly gesticulating hands were telling a silent story she couldn't quite interpret. Clint seemed to be keeping up, though, and he gifted Leighton with his absolute, undivided interest.

Romy's chest squeezed, watching how her son ate up the attention. How he blossomed. How the two of them were so very comfortable in each other's muddy, mute presence.

Lord, what would it be like to feel comfortable around Clint McLeish? And what would that gentle gaze feel like if it was fluttering down on her instead of her son? It was a side of him she'd never seen.

It was a side of *any* man she'd never seen.

Instinctively she knew that he could be gentle. He

would be gentle. In-between intimidating the heck out of her. The sudden fantasy of those enormous, mud-covered hands tracing over her skin took her by surprise. Her body physically jerked as though fingers really were sliding over her shoulders, or learning the lower curve of a breast. Her breath came out in short puffs.

Whoa—desperate much, Carvell?

Clint turned and his eyes found hers amongst the trees and locked on hard. He might as well have sensed her X-rated thoughts. Their burning regard held her frozen where she stood and her breath died mid-fill even as her heart thundered. The green depths were unfathomable but steady and sure, holding a promise. A question.

Romy wasn't sure she wanted to know the answer.

'Leighton.' His words were for the boy by his side but his eyes stayed glued to Romy's. Leighton turned to where she stood in the trees. His cheeks coloured.

'Mum…'

Uh-oh. That was not his happy voice. She cleared her throat. 'Leighton, you didn't ask to come down here. You have homework.'

'Not now, Mum.'

Romy's eyebrows shot up with her tension levels. Here we go… 'Leighton. Home. Now.'

He turned back to the frogs. 'Later.'

Clint's eyes hadn't left hers. Romy was critically aware of their intense focus, of the expectation live in them. She was his security coordinator. She *had* to manage her son.

'I won't ask again…' Her heart thudded painfully. Her father's words spilling out of her mouth. She felt the rising anger of a parent being challenged in the same breath as she relived the memories of a child sick to death of battles. Her gut tightened.

His little body didn't so much as move.

'Leighton Carvell…get your butt back up to the house.'

This time he moved, but only to turn his head back over his shoulder and glare at her. That expression was so familiar. It was her own from twelve years ago.

'Or what?' He frowned.

She saw Clint's eyebrows lift, just slightly. *Crap!* She didn't want to do this. She didn't want to threaten Leighton. Or mess with his mind. Or, God forbid, get physical. But Clint was measuring every move she made.

She went for threat.

'Or I call Carolyn Lawson and say the sleepover is off.' Her voice shook enough that nobody could miss it. Clint's narrowed eyes certainly hadn't.

Leighton scrambled around and up onto angry feet and screamed at her. 'Hangout!'

Deep breaths, Romy. 'Whatever. It's off if you don't get back up to the house and start your science homework.'

Stupid. Why were they fighting? He was probably learning more here in the boggy gully than fourth-grade science would ever teach. Still those green eyes watched. Assessed.

Leighton finally weighed his options and turned petulant eyes to the man lying still as a stone next to him. He turned the tantrum off in an eye blink. Strategically. ''Bye, Clint.'

Clint's voice was carefully neutral. 'See ya, buddy. We'll do this again.'

Leighton nodded silently and then huffed past Romy, not meeting her eyes. A tight fist clenched around her lungs, but she forced words out as he passed. 'Watch out for that pout, mate. You might trip on it.'

She turned to watch him go. When she trusted that he was genuinely heading for the house she turned back to her boss, humiliated that he'd witnessed the family altercation. He was on his feet, brushing off the loose, damp dirt. 'Sorry about that,' she said on a puff.

'You asked again.' His gaze was steady, half veiled.

'What?'

'Leighton. After telling him you wouldn't ask him again to do his homework, you asked.'

'So? He wasn't getting me.'

'Oh, he was getting you all right. He was ignoring you.'

'Thank you, I'm well aware of that. Am I about to get a parenting lecture?'

'Depends. Do you need one?'

Romy let her mouth drop open. Attractiveness be

damned. 'You knowing so much about parenting, of course.'

His eyebrows lifted. 'I know something about little boys. Young men. I've trained enough of them. And it looks like I know a hell of a lot more than you about maintaining discipline.'

Romy settled both fists onto her hips. 'Am I getting paid for this?'

It was Clint's turn to look confused. He blinked at her.

'If you're about to give me some skills-development training? Is this on the clock?'

'Romy…'

'Don't tell me how to raise my son!' Her voice echoed through the little gully. Frogs and birds flew for cover in all directions.

Clint kept his cool. 'When you say you're not going to ask again and then you ask, Leighton wins. He'll remember. And he'll use it in his next combat.'

'This is not a war. This is a family. *My* family.' *At least, she was working damn hard to keep it that way.*

'Sometimes there's no difference. It's the same psychology.'

'I prefer a different kind of psychology. One based on love and compassion rather than threats and punishments.'

His laugh was genuine. 'Let me know how that works out for you.'

'He's an eight-year-old child, Clint. Not a soldier.'
Just like she'd been.

'Last time I checked, only one of us has *been* an eight-year-old boy. Trust me on what works for them.'

'Trust *me* on what works for my son.'

He held her gaze, breathing in and out calmly. 'Love and compassion has made Leighton the boy he is. He's a great kid. But he's going to start pushing your buttons more and more. Stretching you. Testing you. Trying to dominate you. I recognise the signs.'

She turned to follow her son up the hill. 'That may be what you were like but it's not Leighton.'

'It's all boys, Romy,' he called after her. 'It's imprinted on us. We're built to try to take charge.'

She spun around. 'If you are so fired up about parenthood why don't you sire a brood of your own? Go bully your own kids.'

He sprinted up the steep slope in three easy steps and swung around in front of her, halting her with a hand on her shoulder. 'Managing your son does not make you a bully.'

She shrugged her shoulder away and glared. 'Well, badgering me makes you one. And I think there's a bunch of workplace laws that protect me from that.'

He dropped his hand and ran it through his thick hair. 'Romy. I'm not trying to get under your skin—'

She stalked off, around him. 'You *do not* get under my skin.'

Liar.

'I just want to help you,' he called after her. 'Use some of what I've learned over the years.'

She turned back around and glared at him from the actual—and moral—high ground. 'Well, Sensei, this little grasshopper is not interested in your wax-on-wax-off wisdom. Thanks all the same.'

He swore as she carried on up the gully, and then shouted an order after her. 'We're still on for tomorrow afternoon.'

She just held up an angry hand and scrambled, shaking, up the path to safety.

'Ready to go?'

After a night of angry stewing and then a day of having to force her mind to stay on the job, Romy was more than ready. The faster they got started, the faster she'd be back home. She turned to where Clint stood in her doorway. 'I'm not sure this qualifies as afternoon any more. It's closer to evening.'

'I thought I'd stay out of your way while you were working. You looked busy. Besides, you need to see this near dusk to appreciate it.'

He'd watched her working? How, when all her senses were finely tuned to any sign of his arrival? Then again, he was trained in stealth.

'Do I need anything?' She glanced around her spotless kitchen.

'Nope. Just yourself.'

Out of habit, she grabbed her rucksack and locked the house behind them. Country or not, she would hand in her security licence before she'd leave it open to anyone passing, even with Leighton out for the night at Cameron's. Clint waited patiently by his ute until she was done securing her home.

Her plan to remain detached and disinterested lasted about twenty-five seconds. The sight of all six foot four of him leaning casually against his vehicle waiting for her excited her pulse.

Relax, it's only a drive. Not looking at him would make this much easier. She climbed in and fixed her focus out the front windscreen. 'Where are we going?'

'We've had reports about trafficking activity in the area. Cockatoos and reptiles. I wanted you to see WildSprings's roosting sites so you know what to be watching for.'

'This is about the Customs memo?' She had received a copy as well. 'I didn't realise it affected us here.'

'It might not. But it's about cockatoo theft and we have one of the best feeding sites of red-tails in the region. And some nests. That makes us a target.'

Romy snapped straight into work mode. 'So this is precautionary?' She glanced at him from the passenger seat and noticed a dark bruise twisting around his throat. It looked nasty. Her muscles tensed. 'What happened to you?'

His hand automatically rose to the mark, then waved it off. 'Sporting injury.'

Oh, really? 'What kind of sport does that to you?'

His attention flicked from the road to her, then back again. 'Deep caving.'

Romy stared. Exploring the abundant natural pores of the earth in the south-west of Australia was a particularly dangerous pastime. Every now and again the caves took payment in the form of human lives. Her stomach fluttered. 'You can't watch the footy like the rest of Australia?'

Clint smiled. 'I like football. But I love caving. There's something about the silence. The darkness. Going somewhere virtually no-one else has been.'

The heart-stopping danger. 'You can stand in the bush and get dark silence.'

'Not quite the same.'

'What other questionable pastimes do you have?'

'I own a good movie collection and I'm learning to love paperback mysteries.'

'Hmm…and when you're not escaping into popular culture?'

He stared at the road ahead, holding out.

'Come on, McLeish. 'Fess up.'

'I kite-surf,' he said finally.

Romy nodded, straight-faced. 'Challenging.'

'And I abseil.'

'Oh, now you're just showing off. So that's below ground, terrestrial and marine sports covered. Surely you must base-jump off mountains or something. Bungee?'

His smile broke free. 'I've been known to jump

out of helos.' At her frown he clarified. 'Military choppers.'

'Of course you have.' She shook her head.

'What?'

'You're an adrenaline junkie. I'm struggling to fit the man who likes silence and privacy and classic movies with the man who surfs whales and wrangles wild boar with his bare hands.'

That sinful mouth twitched. 'Well, not *bare* hands...'

She laughed but it was hollow, even to her own ears. Clint McLeish missed the rush that came with doing his duty. The risk. Living with death daily. She could only imagine how a body would become accustomed to being hyper-aroused for survival, how hard it must be to kick the habit. 'How much combat have you seen?'

The relaxed smile died and his hands tightened around the steering wheel. 'Even if I wanted to talk about it, which I don't—' he glanced at her '—most everything I saw during my service is confidential. I couldn't discuss it with you.'

With me. The implication twisted in her gut. The line in the sand got more defined. Clint, boss. Romy, staff. It was just a little too close to a childhood full of alienation in the name of military confidence. 'Do you jump out of aircrafts and climb into the sphincters of the earth as a way of re-creating your time in the military? Or forgetting it?'

His face grew hard. 'It's a hobby, Romy. People have them.'

Her eyebrows lifted. 'I have hobbies, but they're not quite as extreme as yours. Isn't there anything more… ordinary…that interests you?'

The shadowed bruise on his throat shifted as his Adam's apple lurched upwards. She'd pushed him too far….

'I like to cook. Since I came here.'

If he'd said he liked to make candles from earwax, she couldn't have been more surprised. She gaped at him. 'Really? What kinds of things?'

He shrugged. 'Whatever. Cordon bleu. Cajun. Armenian. Anything new.'

Romy looked out the side window, reining in a chuckle she knew would get her in trouble.

'What? Why stop sharing your thoughts now?' His sarcasm was barely contained.

'That's extreme cooking.' Her laugh bubbled out. 'You really suck the marrow out of life, don't you, McLeish?'

He looked annoyed. 'I don't do it to be adventurous.'

'Why do you do it?'

The silence fell between them like autumn leaves. His eyes blazed. The ute's old dash clock ticked.

'Just to feel something.'

She stared at him. A moment ago she'd been envious of the man who lived a no-fear life. Imagining how good that would feel. Now, suddenly, she was responding to the raw awkwardness in his eyes. Clint McLeish and his emotions didn't spend a lot of time communing, it seemed. She opened her mouth to ask him more.

'We're here.' He pulled the ute off the track near a stand of banksia and marri trees.

The silence of the bush after the conversation in the car was striking. But then Romy heard the raucous, happy grumbling high above. She tilted her head and scanned the thick branches. Once she saw one, more and more came into focus. Enormous black cockatoos with a flame of red on their long sweeping tails, settling in for the night, high in the treetops.

'Is this where they nest?'

He shook his head. 'This is where they roost each night. They have nesting sites scattered all over the region, but Far Reach is a favoured site and generations of red-tails will teach their young to return to this gully to feed and roost as soon as they leave the nest.'

She stared all around, thinking about how deep in the property they were, considering how high in the trees the birds were roosting. Anyone who came here with theft on their mind would have some hurdles to overcome. That made her job easier.

'Thank you for bringing me. This is important for me to see.'

'These guys are one of the reasons I returned to WildSprings. I consider them my surrogate family. No-one messes with my family.'

She looked at him and believed it. Even removed

from his military context there was still something inherently dangerous about the way he moved, the way he assessed everything around him. The way he missed nothing. She wouldn't want to cross him.

'Why don't you have a family of your own?' The question slipped out before she'd really thought about the ramifications.

He glanced at her. 'Women and children are a bit thin on the ground around here in case you hadn't noticed.'

'I'm sure there'd be a few bold contenders in town prepared to put up with your surly stares.' Was that a smile? Hard to tell—it morphed into a determined frown way too quickly.

'I guess I'm not family material.' He shrugged.

Her snort was critically unladylike. 'Are you serious? You're a born provider, you're practically the kid whisperer and you'd look good at any parent-and-teacher night fighting them off with a stick.' She blushed furiously at what she'd just admitted. She cleared her throat. 'So…shall we head back?'

He watched her for a moment, followed her glance out to the darkening skies, then turned for the ute. Romy threw one final look into treetops littered with black-feathered shapes. To the wrong sort of mind, they would look like plump wads of cash growing on trees.

Her planned perimeter checks mentally doubled.

'The kid whisperer, huh?' He started the ute.

'You don't think so?'

'I'm not very…comfortable with children. Haven't had a lot of positive experiences.'

'Well, they like you. Leighton does, anyway. He's practically got a crush.'

There. That twist of full lips was unquestionably a smile.

She slid into the passenger seat and risked a glance at Clint's unreadable profile. Stirring him was a little bit like poking a lion with a stick. Really not advised. But he was smiling, not snarling. Despite his closed-off concentration on the road, she'd never felt safer.

The novelty of the thought brought her head up. Since Leighton came, her job was to make sure *he* was okay. To work hard to create a haven for them both. But it had been a long time since she'd felt like this. Safe. As though she could simply let go of all the responsibility, just for a moment, and someone else would take it on.

Her brows came together. Had she ever felt safe? Before giving birth, her childhood was one big shadow, with the dominant, angry figure of the Colonel front and centre. Colonel Martin Carvell specialised in order, discipline and results. Three things most young children instinctively repelled. He found it impossible to hide his dissatisfaction with every aspect of her performance as his only offspring, so he embraced it, taking her on as his personal project. Which, of course, she was. He fathered her. In the absence of her mother who died so young, who else's responsibility would she be?

Unfortunately for her, the Colonel was as zealous with her improvement as he had been over a lifetime of whipping raw recruits into good military material. His favoured tools of the trade were a firm hand and harsh tongue. Romy still carried the emotional scars both had left her with. Above all was the lingering sense that she was *insufficient*. No matter what she did it would never be quite good enough.

And now it looked as if Clint McLeish was harbouring similar thoughts. That somehow—though he didn't yet know how—she was going to stuff up. Like the failure her father always told her she was.

She let her gaze drift to the road in front of them. They narrowed.

What the…?

'Stop!' Romy flung out her hands to brace herself on the windscreen as the word exploded from her lips. In the same moment, Clint slid the ute sideways as his foot slammed the brake hard to the floor. The engine stalled. The only sound was the blood rushing furiously past her ears. Then breath returned and she burst into action.

Across the middle of the track, a large western grey kangaroo lay mortally wounded. Its head jerked uselessly in the gravel and Romy's heart lurched painfully. She reached for the first-aid kit, unclipped her seatbelt and pushed the door open all in the same manoeuvre.

She was on her feet and rushing towards the injured animal before Clint had fully registered what was going on, but he still managed to be there ahead of her. The moment she got to its side, strong arms wrapped around her and dragged her back from the injured creature.

'Romy, no. Just wait!'

'For what? It needs help.'

'She could kill you with those legs. Look at her feet.'

She'd never noticed how savage the claws on the end of a kangaroo's huge feet were. But the rest of the animal…

'I don't think she can even move.'

He stared at the critical animal and released her. She found her feet and moved towards the kangaroo more cautiously. He was right beside her. Blood trickled from the poor creature's nose and its eyes rolled at the approach of humans. But its injuries were extensive and the stillness of the rest of the lean, grey body was ominously telling.

Clint saw it, too. 'Her spine's broken.'

She kneeled at the roo's side and gently stroked its furred shoulder, tears biting. The kangaroo's wide-eyed stare wheeled around to what she was doing but there was no sign it could feel a thing. Her heart ached for its suffering.

'Go back to the car.' Clint's voice was firm.

She looked up at the bleak shadows turning his green eyes stormy. 'No. There must be something we can—'

'Leave her with me. It's kinder this way.'

He was nearly as grey as the roo, now. It dawned on her what he was going to do. Her heart clenched. 'No, you can't…'

Dark eyes turned on her. 'I'm trained to kill, Romy. It's what I do best. Now will you please go back to the car?'

Torn between wanting to stay with him while he did the unthinkable and knowing she wouldn't be able to watch, she shuffled to his side. Just being closer to him made things that tiny bit better.

'Romy.' His voice softened but his bleak gaze appealed. 'Every second you're stubborn is a second longer this animal is suffering.'

She dipped her head and turned away, shamed. As she did, a tragic hiss came from behind her. She and Clint both looked at the roo, where nature had finally taken care of its own.

In the pause between heartbeats, all signs of life vanished.

Her tears turned to relief. For the kangaroo and for Clint, who seemed so stoically resigned to killing it. She glanced down at the animal and watched the slight movements of its abdomen settling into death.

'Romy—' urgency filled Clint's voice '—in the tray of the ute is my old training sweater. Can you grab it, please?'

He knelt in front of the dead roo and she hurried to find what he'd asked for. As she crossed to the vehicle, she noticed a set of tracks in the earth—disturbance where they'd skidded and then driven on again around the roo. She glanced at the ute's tyres. Wrong profile. She grabbed her mobile phone as she reached into the ute for Clint's old sweater.

He was hunched over the kangaroo's corpse when she returned and she passed him the sweater, unable to look at the unseeing eyes. As soon as her hands were free, she turned back to the tire tracks, flipped open her phone and took a photograph of the distinctive tread marks, focusing determinedly on finding out who'd been here just before them. Somebody with expensive tires had been in the park this evening. At speed, judging by the distance from impact to where the roo lay.

Careless yahoos.

'Romy, can you help me?'

She closed the notepad and turned carefully towards Clint, unsure exactly what he was asking for. What she saw nearly floored her. He extracted a tiny, damp, furred bundle from the pouch of the stricken kangaroo. A joey. That was what she'd seen moving so slightly in the mother's body. He tucked it immediately into the warmth of the sweater and used the sleeves to tie around Romy's neck like a sling.

She stood quietly, staring in amazement at the large, confused eyes which blinked at her from the deep folds of fabric. The joey immediately sought the warmth of her body, settling in the makeshift pouch and pressing harder against her heartbeat. Clint leaned in close, reaching behind to fashion a knot from the stretched sleeves. In moments it was done and she found herself a surrogate mother to the tiniest life she'd ever held.

Her gaze drifted up and found Clint's. From death to life in a heartbeat. Her energy shifted from mourning the dead kangaroo to the survival of her tiny joey. His own eyes burned with focus, as though the opportunity to save a life consumed him.

'Climb in. There's a carer about an hour away. We'll take her there.'

'Her?'

'Look at her eyes—they're enormous like yours.' His regard burned into her for the briefest of moments, the barest suggestion of the simmering, molten man behind the tough exterior. It was enough to make Romy's mouth dry.

First feeling safe. Now going pasty mouthed. What the hell was coming over her?

As Clint dragged the dead roo's carcass gently to the side of the track, she climbed in the front seat of the ute and secured the tiny life form more firmly against her body. She wasn't too concerned about its ability to breathe. A woollen sweater would have to be easier than the thick damp cover of a flesh pouch.

She patted the mobile phone in her pocket to make sure it was still there and then turned to Clint.

'Drive.'

CHAPTER FIVE

WITHOUT the little life pressed against her chest, Romy felt strangely cold.

They'd interrupted the carer sitting to dinner with her family but on seeing their precious bundle the whole family kicked into action, apparently well used to the arrival of pouch-age survivors of roo strikes. Before Romy and Clint left, the carer's husband took a moment to introduce some other young kangaroos, all raised by their family, all survivors of road accidents. Seeing them so healthy and grown was the only reason Romy was willing to leave her tiny charge in their very good hands. Otherwise, she was going to ask for a crash course in marsupial raising and take the baby home again.

Clint had to shepherd her with his body away from the joey as it settled in a lamb's-wool pouch in the arms of the carer, hungrily slurping rescue formula from a baby's bottle. There was nothing more they could do, but she'd been strangely reluctant to go. It was stupid, but it felt like *their* joey—hers and Clint's.

All the more reason to leave it behind, she thought

now, staring out into the thick darkness of the forest as they drove. The last thing she needed was additional reasons to feel connected to a self-confessed hermit. And an ex-military one at that. She sighed.

'People suck.' Given they were the first real words she'd uttered in the forty-minute return trip, they held some weight.

Clint turned to look at her, his eyes glowing in the light coming off the dash. 'Can't disagree with that. Why particularly?'

'That roo was just minding her own business, getting her baby somewhere safe for the night, and…wham!' They weren't called *roo bars* for nothing. Most country vehicles had them. Great for protecting the fronts of cars, not so great for the hapless roos they connected with.

'We saved one life tonight. That's something.'

She sighed deeply. 'Doesn't feel like enough.'

His voice dropped to husky. 'You have a soft centre, Romy Carvell.'

She snorted. 'Yeah, I'm a regular Turkish delight.'

His lips twisted as he returned to watching the road. 'Maybe you have to have seen the loss of life to appreciate saving one.'

Romy glanced at him. 'Maybe so. I've never had anyone close to me die. Not that I remember.'

He glanced at her. 'Grandparents?'

'Nope. Gone pre-me.'

'Parents?'

'Mum died having me. Dad's still around.' *Somewhere*.

'Consider yourself lucky, then.'

'You've seen a fair bit of death.' Not a question.

'Seen it.' He took his eyes off the road for longer to stare at her. 'Been it.'

She chuckled. 'Now I'm imagining you getting around in a hooded cape with a sickle.'

'It felt like it some days.'

Her voice softened. 'It would take a lot of saved kangaroos to offset that, I would imagine.'

He thought about that. 'Not so many. Death is a process. Life is a miracle. Saving even one means something.'

They passed through the WildSprings entry statement and Romy instinctively glanced around for any signs of trouble. Hard habit to break. She noticed Clint did the same. As they reached the admin building, Justin emerged with an armful of files, heading for his 4WD. He raised his free hand in a wave. Clint responded with the obligatory country salute, a couple of fingers lifted from the steering wheel.

She glanced at her watch, wondering why Justin was working so late and gasped. 'It's ten o'clock! I didn't ring Leighton.' It was too late to call now; the boys would probably be in bed.

'He'll be fine. Call in the morning.'

Being managed irritated her as much as the fact that Clint was once again giving her parenting advice. She reached for her mobile. 'What if he needs me?'

He slid his hand over hers to prevent her from flipping her phone open. 'Then he would have called you. Seriously, Romy. Let him enjoy a night away.'

Away from me? She measured her words before uttering them. 'You think I overprotect him.'

'I think you've done an amazing job with him…'

But…

'…but he's growing up and he's going to start needing some space from Mum now and again.'

Romy knew he was right, but she didn't like having it pointed out by a virtual stranger. *No,* her inner voice condemned. She may have only met him a week ago but Clint McLeish was less of a stranger than the small handful of people she'd known her whole life. He just seemed to…get her.

'Are you speaking from personal experience? Did you value your space even as a kid?' she asked.

He looked at her, surprised. 'I guess I did, yes. I was eight before my brother came along, so I learned early to entertain myself.'

A younger brother. No wonder he knew how little boys could be. He'd watched one growing up.

'What happened to your parents?' Romy knew he owned WildSprings outright. Had they died?

'They split after twenty-five years together.' He coughed. 'Mum met someone else. She moved to the US around about the same time I enlisted.'

Wow. 'What happened to your brother?'

'He was only ten. He went with her to America.'

She watched the tension play out across his features

and tried to imagine how that would have divided a son's loyalties, even a nearly grown one. 'That must have been hard.'

He shrugged. 'It made me a prime catch for the Taipans. The most effective operators have little or no family ties. Nothing to come home to. Nothing to hold them back on missions.'

Nothing to live for?

'With his whole family gone Dad didn't really have a good reason to stay. He sold up half the land to a neighbour and joined his brothers in Tasmania on the proceeds. He signed the remaining property over to me. To give me somewhere to come home to.'

'To an empty house?' Romy didn't have to like him to empathise with that.

Clint's smile was grim. 'I only came here because it was empty. I was no fit company back then.'

She risked poking the stick a bit further in, her curiosity piqued. 'Why not?'

Like an angry sea anemone, he shut down before her eyes. 'Don't interrogate me, Romy.'

Whoops, too far.

She sighed. 'You should really get out with people more often, McLeish. Your social skills could do with some polishing.'

She turned to stare out into the darkness. The silence was hardly golden. The fork in the track separating her house from Clint's came up in the headlights. He slowed the ute to turn.

'What are you doing?' Her head snapped around.

'I'm following your advice. Getting out with people more often. I'm taking you to my place.'

The lurch of anticipation in her chest was warning enough. She could not be alone with him in his house. Not while she was so emotionally raw from the evening's events. She needed fortification before she tackled this. 'No, you're not!'

He read the panic in her voice. Glanced at her. 'You've never seen my house. You'd like it.'

'I'd like it in the daytime just as much.'

'I'm talking about a short visit, Romy. Grabbing something to eat. As your growling stomach keeps reminding me, I kept you out through dinner.'

Embarrassed, she pressed an hand to her belly. But being so close to him all evening had triggered a different kind of appetite altogether. And she absolutely, categorically, could not hunger for this man.

'I have food at my house. Take me home, please.' The tightness in her whole body seeped out through her words.

He slowed the car to the side of the track and dropped it back to a quiet idle. He turned in the seat and pinned her with his eyes, a deep frown cutting over them. 'Romy, I'm talking about a simple meal between colleagues. Nothing loaded.'

She stared at him boldly. 'Simple? I bet you've never shared a meal at home with a colleague in your life.'

His gaze fell away briefly. 'All the more reason to break the cycle. We'll just eat together. I don't know...

talk.' He gestured helplessly. 'I can work on my people skills.'

The reluctance in his expression helped her to relax. It seemed entirely genuine. Could two people want to spend time together *less*? Her lips quirked slightly. 'You'll make something normal to eat?'

He laid his large hand over the left side of his chest in a pledge. 'No extreme cooking.'

Her breath caught at the intensity in his eyes, despite his light manner. *Colleagues.* Someone needed to remind her body of that, the way it was straining to lean closer to him. 'Okay. Sorry to have overreacted.'

He looked at her seriously. 'You weren't wrong about my people skills—I *am* out of practice. I should have asked. Again.'

'You should have, yes.'

His burning gaze threatened to flame right over her. 'Romy Carvell, would you like to have a meal with me? See my house? No strings attached?'

Amazingly, the answer, now he was actually asking instead of telling, was yes. She nodded.

'Thank you.' He cranked the ute into gear and bumped off along the track.

In less than two minutes, they were there. Her breath caught high in her chest at the first sight of his infamous tree house. It was aptly named.

Built around majestic tree trunks, the timber-and-glass house seemed to grow out of the forest surrounding it. Light glowed invitingly inside and he parked the ute right beneath its sprawling supports. Moments later she climbed the timber staircase leading into the house.

'This is amazing. You built it?' Since when did military training encompass this level of construction skill?

'It's part kit home and part architect modified. I got assistance in as I needed it, but otherwise I constructed it myself.'

'It took two years?' He'd said something about living in her cottage for that long.

'I wanted to get it right.'

She looked around at the open-plan sensation as he swung the entry door inwards. The two enormous tree trunks seemed to push through the floor and extend way up to a high-pitched roof. The entire front wall was glass, framed by more timber. It looked out onto the same view as Leighton's window but from the other end of the gully.

She was almost speechless. 'You did get it right. This is beautiful.'

The place oozed sanctuary. The mix of natural materials, space and light was healing all in itself. She turned to look at him. 'You should be really proud of this.'

The tiniest hint of colour formed where the hard angle of his jaw started. When he flipped a light switch, huge floodlights came on outside, illuminating the trees that surrounded them. Romy gasped. Two dozen glowing eyes blinked back at them, reminding her of pink Christmas lights.

'Can we turn it off?' She crossed to the glass doors opening onto the deck, loath to disturb the possums' nocturnal wanderings. 'I love the darkness at WildSprings.'

Were there even more stars visible from this side of the gully? Impossible, of course, but they seemed to blanket the sky. She tucked her arms in against the coolness of the night and tipped her face to the twinkling brilliance.

He followed her outside, stood chest to shoulder with her. Silent. Strong. The darkness and silence were his friends, too, she remembered.

Just colleagues. The words echoed in her brain, demanding to be heeded. But as the warmth from his body reached out to her and the fragrance of the night bush mingled with his scent, she had to fight to keep them in focus.

Colleagues. She swallowed and stepped away. 'Do you mind if I look around?'

'Help yourself. I'll get something cooking. Spaghetti bolognaise pedestrian enough for you?'

She sighed on a smile. Leighton didn't like pasta so she hardly ever made it. The chance to enjoy real bolognaise on a dinner plate instead of on toast from a tin was hard to knock back. 'It sounds wonderful. Thank you.'

Clint busied himself in the kitchen and Romy took the opportunity to put some distance between them. She padded up the sweeping timber steps to the second storey and tiptoed along the corridor. Immediately on her right was the master bedroom. She averted her gaze and pushed past, not ready to intrude into his personal space but not able to say why. She started at the far end of the hall.

The first door she tried was a bathroom, simply but tastefully decorated with an oversize glass shower recess. No bath. That didn't surprise her in the slightest. Clint McLeish didn't strike her as a soaker. He was all business. Get in dirty, get out clean. *Wham, bam, thank you, ma'am.* She, on the other hand, liked nothing better as a rare treat than to light a bunch of candles after Leighton had gone to bed and soak until the water turned cold in her old claw-foot bath. The getting clean part was an incidental bonus.

Mind you, they probably didn't make baths big enough that could comfortably contain a man Clint's size. The impromptu thought was too close to imagining him in *her* claw-foot bath, and so she shut the thought away with a firm click of the bathroom door behind her.

The next room was a small study, significantly less tidy than the rest of the house. Computer, desk, wall-to-ceiling bookshelves, mixed art pieces, stuff everywhere. Much more like most of the rooms at her place.

Across the hall, a spare room with a single bed and simple decoration. Some basic weight-training gear leaned against the wall. A distant part of her wondered why a man who never had visitors bothered to hide his clutter away in the study.

Romy returned to the first door she'd encountered. The master bedroom. She froze. *It's only a room... Stick your head in and then head downstairs. Simple!*

Right. But, oh, she was curious. You could tell a lot about a person by their bedroom. If you had questions...

She nudged the door with her shoulder, glancing self-consciously behind her. The sounds of occupied clanking from the kitchen encouraged her to continue. By far the most dominant feature in the room was a low-profile, king-size bed with a rich charcoal bedspread. Entirely practical for a man of Clint's height but there was something so...decadent...about the size and shape of it. Any bed she could sleep in lengthways, widthways or diagonally was all right in her book. It was far too easy to imagine herself stretched out on it.

And not necessarily alone.

She spun around, her feet moving silently on the woollen rug. A bank of built-in wardrobes lined one wall and Clint had positioned a couple of oversize armchairs in the corner for good measure. Everything was just...big. Romy suddenly felt like tiny Jack in the beanstalk story, sneaking through the giant's palace in search of the golden goose.

As she had the thought, a golden glint on the far wall caught her eye. A small, framed curiosity was perfectly mounted in a prominent position. On the left, a silver sword flanked by two snakes with the motto *Morte prima di disonore* scrolled across the bottom. *Death before dishonour.* The symbol of Strike Force Taipan. That's where she'd recognised his tattoo from. The insignia and others like it had practically wallpapered the Colonel's living room wall.

Mounted to the right of the badge was a red ribbon with a gold star embedded in flames. Her breath died. Not Australia's highest military honour, but it was one of its rarest.

'It's a Commendation for Gallantry.'

At the deep voice right behind her, she spun around, embarrassed to be caught snooping. But Clint's attention was on the flaming star, not on her.

'I know,' she whispered. 'For acts of conspicuous gallantry in action, in circumstances of great peril.' Her mumbled words won his attention back. Instead of times tables, the Colonel had forced her to learn all of Australia's medals, awards and commendations by rote.

He spoke just as she did. 'How do you know this stuff?'

'What did you do to earn this?'

Neither wanted to answer. They stared at each other in silence. Clint finally broke it, opening his mouth with a terse, 'Spaghetti's ready.'

She let herself be led out and down the stairs until her feet floated on the heavenly fragrance of real Italian sauce. She drifted towards the set table and searched around for something to say as they tucked into the pasta. Something to end the awkward silence.

'So what's Justin Long's story?'

Clint eyed her over an enormous forkful of pasta, paused halfway to his mouth. 'What do you mean?'

'He's young, to be managing a place like this.'

'This coming from you?' It wasn't unfriendly. In fact, there was something decidedly warming about being gently teased. It created a charged kind of friction. It felt good.

'I have good instincts about people. He doesn't seem entirely…comfortable…in his role. Like a suit that doesn't fit.'

Clint stared at her. 'Interesting. What else?'

Romy shrugged. 'He doesn't like me.'

It was only a mouthful of food that prevented him bursting into laughter. After a moment he mumbled, 'Half the staff don't like you, according to you.'

'He genuinely doesn't. Since day one. It practically oozes from his pores.'

Clint shrugged. 'It's because I hired you. His nose is out of joint.'

'You're the boss. You can hire whoever you want, can't you?'

Dark eyes studied her. 'It's complicated.'

Romy sighed. 'If I'm going to be able to do my job well I need to know where the skeletons are. You know that.'

He placed his fork down with meticulous care. Took an age, he dabbed his napkin to his lips. 'Justin is my brother.'

It was Romy's turn to splutter. Heat roared up her cheeks. 'What? Since when?'

'Pretty much since birth.'

'Ha-ha. Were you planning on telling me or were you just going to let me keep talking about him.'

'I'm telling you now.'

There was no way a man with his training could possibly miss her simmering expression. Which mean she was being *managed* again. Romy took a deep breath. 'Why have you not mentioned this before?'

'It's not pertinent.'

'It most certainly is. Familial relationships in workplaces increase the likelihood of crime statistically, did you know that? Second only to romantic ones.'

He looked unimpressed. 'Thanks for the intel. But this is a family business. He's the last person I'd be concerned about ripping me off.'

'How long has he worked for you?'

'Is this a social question or a professional one?' His careless tone screamed a warning. He kept his eyes artificially lowered.

Romy took a breath. Backed down. 'Social.' *Gut instinct or not.* 'I'm interested.'

His grunt wasn't convinced. 'Mum took Justin to the US when she left. He lived there until he was nineteen. Then he…wanted to come home.'

Romy frowned. 'He left your mum?'

'We grow up, Romy. We all move away from our mothers eventually. Even Leighton will.'

He was changing the subject. Romy's sensed it instantly.

'Back to Justin... So he came home to WildSprings and you made him business manager?'

'He'd been an assistant concierge in a big hotel in Chicago. He had the right skills and I wasn't interested in running the place then. I'd just got back. I asked him to stay on.'

The word *then* struck her hard. She filed it away. 'What hotel?'

'I don't know. I don't care. Something French. Something big.'

'You must trust him a lot. To give him the job on face value.'

Dark eyes burned into hers. 'You don't?'

No-one messes with my family. The warning echoed in her mind. She shrugged and made her expression nonchalant. 'I'm just making conversation.'

'He really bothers you, doesn't he?' He pushed his half-empty plate away. 'He's my brother, Romy. Of course I trust him. And I owe him—'

If he hadn't cut himself off so sharply, Romy might have let it go. 'Owe him how?'

His face closed down right in front of her. Starting with his eyes and ending with the tightening of his mouth. 'I can't see how that has any bearing on park security.'

Romy's heart banged painfully on her chest wall. She sat back. Dark eyes glared at her and he tipped his head. Subject closed.

For the next ten minutes they ate in silence, a thousand uncomfortable miles apart. So much for a civilised meal between colleagues. Romy's mind worked overtime. Brothers. Oh, joy, that wasn't going to be any fun to get in the middle of. She had no personal experience with siblings but she'd seen them at school, swinging between fiercely fighting and fiercely defending one another. Obviously a complicated relationship, growing up with someone.

How long would it take for the family issue to raise its head? The vibes she was getting off Justin Long guaranteed it would be coming up sooner or later. And she'd be square in the middle of it.

Romy caught Clint's gaze on her a number of times but she dropped hers quickly to mask her thoughts. He was as efficient an eater as he was in everything else and he wiped his plate clean long before Romy did. She realised the error almost immediately. He'd finished and had nothing to do but stare. She was still eating and could hardly hint at going home while food sat on her plate.

Steady eyes considered her. 'Who was he?'

She lifted her eyes, swallowing carefully. 'Who?'

'The man in your life who taught you to—' he changed tack '—who taught you so much about the Defence Force.'

Romy stiffened. 'Why does there have to be a man? Perhaps I'm really interested in Australia's military history.'

'Are you?'

She sighed. She couldn't lie to those eyes. 'No.'

'How long were you together?'

It would be so easy to let him go on thinking it was some other man who had been in the military. It would probably be smart. But those eyes, again…

'It was my father.'

For the first time since she met him, he looked genuinely surprised. 'Your father? I thought… You seemed so…'

'You thought I was running from a failed relationship?' He didn't need to nod. 'I guess in a way I am. But not a romantic one.'

She hadn't been with anyone since the night Leighton was conceived. But she was hardly going to tell him that.

'What branch was he?'

Here came the inevitable. Romy sighed. 'He's a colonel in the army.'

She saw the very moment Clint made the connection. His eyebrows shot up. 'Colonel Martin Carvell is your father?'

Under his inquisitive gaze Romy felt all of sixteen again.

Clint whistled. 'He's a legend in the Defence Force.'

He *was* capable of being impressed, then. Just not by her. Her smile tightened and she pushed the remainder of her food away. 'I'm sure he is. He lived and breathed the army.'

Those sharp green eyes missed nothing. 'But you're running from him?'

'He wasn't much of a legend as a father. I had no interest in raising my son around his influence.' She saw no understanding in his expression. On any other day she would have let it go. Changed the subject. But not with this man. Not tonight. She wanted him to understand.

She nailed him with her eyes. 'Do you remember your basic training?'

His scoff was immediate. 'How could I forget? It was hell.'

'How old were you?'

'Eighteen.'

Romy nodded. Paused. 'Imagine being five.'

She stood, collected both their plates and took them to the kitchen where they clattered as she dropped them into the sink. She cursed. His focus was on her the whole way. Clint's spaghetti was the best she'd ever had but it congealed like concrete in her suddenly churning stomach. She busied herself with scraping off the scraps into his compost tub and rinsing the bowls, blinking furiously.

Out of nowhere, his large hands slid over hers, stilling their fevered activity. His body pressed against her and he spoke behind her ear. 'Leave it, Romy.'

She froze immediately and let him pull the dishes out of her wet, trembling hands. He took one into his own large one and pulled her towards the deck. She stumbled along behind him, sick with the grief of her childhood memories. Recalling vividly what that harsh discipline had felt like to someone not old enough to understand the words, let alone the reason.

Outside, he dropped her hand and she clung to the balustrade for support, breathing deeply. She'd never let herself even *think* about those days, never mind talk about them. It hurt too much. She started suturing up the bursts in her protective layer. Double-reinforcing the leaks.

'Don't,' he said.

She glanced at him warily. 'Don't what?'

'Don't shove it all down again. Don't try and hide it from me. Or from yourself.'

The pain had to go somewhere. She rounded it back onto him, furiously. 'Uh, pot…kettle…black!'

He kept the anger well contained, although she saw it flirting at the edges of his expression. 'It's because I know so much about it that I don't want to see you do it to yourself.'

She fumed silently, recognising the truth.

'How old were you when you left?' he asked.

Facts were so much easier to deal with than feelings. 'Nearly twenty.'

His face tipped towards hers. 'So Leighton was… nearly two?'

'He wouldn't let me leave before that.' She shoved those memories down deep, too. The misery of being trapped with a man she hated while a life grew in her frightened teen belly, then trying to protect herself and her infant son from the Colonel's influence for two years. Her horror when, after barely acknowledging Leighton's existence since his birth, her father had suddenly realised he had a boy-child in the house and began paying attention. The awful day he brought home a toy gun for *the little soldier*. Started making plans for his future. That same day, Romy looked up available support services online. It was the best thing the Colonel had ever done for her.

Even the darkness didn't disguise Clint's reaction. The flash of fury. 'He hurt you?'

She dropped her eyes. 'Define hurt?'

'Did he touch you?'

'Some things are more painful than a thrashing. And his precious code of honour meant he drew a line at beating a pregnant woman.'

Clint stared at her, assessing. 'But before that?'

Pity mingled with compassion in his eyes and pain lanced through her. She was nobody's charity case. She pushed away from the balustrade and turned for the door, blinking back tears. 'Before that, I was a recruit to be broken by whatever means he saw fit.'

He moved quickly but she was quicker, fuelled by hurt and anger. She got halfway to the front door before he spun her back, into the wall of his chest. She resisted the bolt of pleasure that shot through her on feeling his arms around her.

'Romy, I can't let you go like this. So upset. Not to an empty house.'

'I'm not your responsibility.'

He slid his hands over her shoulders and framed her

face on both sides, forcing her to meet his eyes. 'Stay and talk with me. Just until I know you're okay.'

She tried to pull away but his easy hold was like a vice. 'I'm fine. Please let me go. Please…' She was holding the tears in check, but barely. *Don't let me cry in front of him.*

Too late.

A fat tear leaked out the corner of one eye and raced down onto her cheek. His thumb caught it and wiped it away. She pressed her lids closed, unable to bear seeing disappointment in his. At her weakness.

Carvells don't cry!

Clint pulled her into his shoulder, threading one hand through her hair and wrapping the other firmly around her waist. 'Ah, Romy…'

She fit against his contours so perfectly he burned to feel the stiffness of her body turn into warm, relaxed flesh. This was his fault. He never should have quizzed her about her past. He'd only done it to get her off the uncomfortable topic of his brother.

'Shh…'

Stroking her seemed to help, and he was masochist enough to appreciate how good it felt to hold her. Just once. He willed his body not to respond to hers, not to drive her any further away than he already had, but it wasn't easy thinking when all he wanted to do was wrap her up in his arms and never let her out.

Bit by bit, her tension softened and almost seemed to shrink in his arms. He kept up the gentle rhythm of his hands, stroking her hair, her back, trailing over her skin. It was impossible to think of her as an employee when she was like this. She was a woman—someone he'd hurt—who needed comfort.

Just comfort.

'Shh…'

His lips pressed against the top of her head briefly. What a jerk. Why had he pushed her about the man in her past? *Because you wanted to know if she was available,* a little voice accused. *To find out if the field was clear.*

At least be honest with yourself if you're not going to be honest with her.

She tipped her face sideways, relaxing more into his hold, and rested her cheek against his shoulder on a half sigh, half sob. His lips found her temple, touched there briefly, then stayed longer than they should have.

She didn't push away.

Her body changed shape slightly in his arms, curling towards him like a kitten drawn to warmth in its sleep. Sweet pleasure started to race through his veins and his breath heated in his lungs. He stroked her hair away from her face and bent towards her damp, flushed skin, placing a kiss on each closed eyelid. Her heartbeat fluttered against his chest like a tiny bird.

It was drugged heaven. It was right for all the wrong reasons.

She stopped breathing and opened her eyes, fixing her smoky focus on his. A hunger he'd not allowed in years surged through him but he forced it back, made himself proceed with caution, assessing the risk before advancing. He bent his face slowly and found the place just south of her earlobe with his lips and then nibbled a trail forward along her jaw. Tasting. Experiencing.

Reconnaissance.

She whimpered but didn't move away. His target was mere inches from him, two perfect lips that parted on a single word as she sagged in his arms.

'Clint…'

That one syllable on her lips hit him in a place he'd forgotten he even had. Deep, deep inside. Did she even notice she'd finally said his name? God, he burned to see how the word tasted on her lips. But she had to *want* this, and not simply because it made her feel better.

'Romy…' His voice was thick with lust, his body screaming for things he hadn't addressed in a long time. 'I'm going to kiss you.'

That sexy mouth twisted in a satisfied smile and her thick voice was almost drowsy with desire. 'You are kissing me, Clint….'

He moved in closer, his mouth scant millimetres from hers, hovering a hair's-breadth from heaven. Her soft breath brushed warmly against his lips.

Just millimetres…

'No. Really kiss you.'

He was aware, at once, of every place her body pushed against his. The softness of her belly where his hips pressed, the sensation of full breasts crushed low against his chest, the angle of her face as she tipped her mouth up to nearly touch his. His body jerked. So very nearly...

'I'm asking, Romy...' His words were mostly a whisper against her lips. 'I'm looking for permission to proceed.'

It was pure instinct. The language that was such a part of him tumbled off his lips unconsciously. Romy's eyes flew open and stark desperation frosted them over. She suddenly found strength and pushed hard against him, staggering away from the kiss he still burned to seal against her lush lips.

'Oh, God...' she choked, backing off. 'What am I...? What are we doing?'

Easy, McLeish. She was like a live grenade. *Sans* pin. He took a step towards her, trying to lessen the distance she'd forced between them. If she bolted out of here now she was just as likely to hurt herself. And possibly never return.

'I think we were about to test the definition of *colleagues,*' he said.

She latched onto that. 'You're my *boss*! I can't do this!'

He held her eye. 'If you can't, that's okay. But don't hide behind the boss thing. The two of us were never going to have a conventional employee-employer relationship. And you know it.'

'No!' Her breasts heaved up and down, hypnotically distracting in his periphery. Clint forced himself to keep his eyes on hers. Her fear was signposted in them.

'I'm a different man, Romy. I'm not him,' he said.

She backed hard into the kitchen bench. He raised his hands carefully to his side to try and lessen the impact of him standing between her and the door. That wasn't going to improve matters.

'You're military!'

'That's what I did. Not who I am.'

She shook her head, her senses returning with a vengeance. 'No. You are every bit military, regardless of how long you've been out of it.'

'That still doesn't make me like him.' Although in his gut he knew it did. In part.

She took a deep breath. 'Take me home.'

He stepped towards her. Her hands came up. 'Romy…'

'Then I'll drive myself, give me the keys.'

'Don't do this…'

'Fine, I'll walk.'

She pushed away from the bench and straight past him, more than ready for a fight. He stepped clear and let her pass, but dogged her heels to the exit and down the outside stairs. He'd led enough men to know when a strategic retreat was required.

Time to regroup and reassess.

'I'll drive you, Romy. And I'll leave you at your door. And I won't so much as touch you again.'

Tonight.

She turned and stared at him through enormous, bright eyes. Great…this is how they got into this mess. He was a sucker for waterworks.

The mile drive was brutal. Neither of them spoke—
no surprise, but he'd never considered his old friend
silence an adversary before. It ate at his nerves as he
pulled up in front of her cottage. He no longer thought
of it as his parents' place, only Romy's.

The moment he yanked on the handbrake, she was
out the door. His father's manners made him step out
of the driver's seat. She turned when she hit the front
verandah.

'This is not about you, Clint,' she disarmed him
by saying, not quite able to meet his eyes. 'But this is
about what you do. Did. I cannot be with a man who
has any part of my father in him. I can't have Leighton
exposed to that. If you can honestly tell me there's no
part of you that's like him, then I'll listen. I swear I
will.'

Her eyes were like dinner plates in her pale face.
Clint thought about his time as an operative. The
good men he'd pushed just short of breaking point.
The things he'd seen…done. And the things he'd been
unable to reconcile himself to. The military was deeply
embedded in his soul and, even now, he struggled to
remember he wasn't about unit, corps, God, country,
any more.

He was nothing like Leighton's grandfather…yet
everything like him.

And so he stayed silent. Even though every part of
him wanted to fight to get back the moment they'd
so very nearly shared. The moment when something
fundamental had shifted in his universe. In his soul.

Instead, he stared silently at her.

She nodded sadly and turned for the house. 'Goodnight, Clint.'

Then she was gone. He slumped in the ute and slammed his hand against the aging dash. He'd spent a lifetime controlling his emotions but it took him more than a minute to get them under command now.

CHAPTER SIX

ANOTHER damaged fence kept Romy busy. As fast as she patched them up, more breaches appeared. Not that being thoroughly occupied was a bad thing, but her already filthy mood wasn't improved any by spending a second afternoon in the Australian sun straining wire.

Stop your whining, girl, and get on with it. She heard the Colonel's hard voice barking at her as though he were right there on the hill. Instinctively she sucked in her breath and straightened her spine. She yanked the final wire tight and stood back to examine her work.

It was getting harder to imagine this was only kids sneaking onto the property for an unauthorised swim or a farmer helping himself to fruit. Simone told her they'd not had breaches like this before so why the difference now? Because she'd sealed up a regular access point when she first arrived? Maybe activity was on the rise? Or could someone be making life intentionally difficult for her? She glanced around. Whichever, she

was determined to solve it. To prove herself to all the
knockers who were waiting for her to mess up.

She tossed her tools into the boot of her car.

Who was she kidding; most of the WildSprings staff
had already accepted her, even if one or two had taken
a while to warm to her. There was only one person she
was trying to prove herself to and he remained entirely
oblivious to her strengths.

She shook her head. Not surprising, really. It seemed
as if all she'd done in Clint's presence was confront
him, disagree or wail like a banshee, all of which
hardly engendered confidence. And then there was
the kissing...

Romy flushed anew remembering how she'd practically climbed inside his skin back in the tree house.
On all of one week's acquaintance. It had felt so right
for those blessed moments before she'd come to her
senses. The fact he'd responded wholeheartedly did
not lessen her embarrassment. Maybe he just hadn't
been to the city for a while?

She knew for certain he went the very next day.

That was ten days ago now and she hadn't so much
as caught a whiff of him since then. He certainly knew
how to lay low. But she'd not had the same success
getting him out of her head. Even now she could still
feel how his body moved under her touch. The hard,
living shelf of flesh over his strong heartbeat, the gentle
scrape of stubble across her cheek, the feathery silk of
his lips on her skin as he whispered comforting sounds
in her ear. And that smell... Her lids fluttered shut.

Stop!

She braced her hands on the hood of her car and took six deep breaths. Nothing good could come from revisiting the incident over and over. Clint McLeish was officially out of bounds.

Despite what the hollow ache in her chest thought.

Did she need a flashing red light to go off every time he got too close? The man was a risk-taker, ex–special services and had closed himself off from the world. He had more baggage than a 747.

Takes one to know one, a tiny voice whispered.

She shot forwards on the track in a spray of dust and sent dirt scattering behind her car. What *was* his baggage all about? All she knew was he'd been a Taipan. And they were at the precision end of encounters in some of the world's hottest war zones. He'd told her himself he'd killed people, but in the context of his regiment maybe that meant he'd *killed* people.

As in up close. Intensely personal. Impossible to forget.

He certainly had the haunted look of a man who'd seen too much. And he'd left that world behind and dug himself an existence here in the forest. He called it somewhere to heal but Romy looked at it as a hole to lie down and die in.

Just like any mortally wounded animal.

Her heart reached out to that part of him. The part she'd glimpsed for barely a moment that night in his house. The part, she very much suspected, that was responsible for framing and mounting his service badge and commendation.

You wouldn't do that if you didn't care. If he didn't, he wouldn't hurt so much. And the flashes in his eyes when she'd asked about it were most definitely pain.

For the first time, she saw a glint of reason to the way the military trained its people. Especially in those kinds of units. You'd need a certain level of psychological shielding in order to strap on a weapon and take human lives. Otherwise, the enormity of the job you had to do might just eat you up.

She frowned. That was how her father had trained. How he lived his life. How he tried to make Romy live hers. What happened to the people who couldn't handle the discipline, who rebelled against the absolutes? Did they go out at seventeen and brand their bodies with vivid symbols of wild, rebellious freedom across their backs? Then get so blisteringly drunk in misery they'd fall into bed with the first person who showed them a hint of compassion?

Maybe they did.

Maybe other people failed the military test with equally spectacular results. She'd gone on to grow into a tough, resilient, capable woman. But that was in spite of her upbringing, not because of it.

She crunched the gears on her vehicle. Family sure had a lot to answer for. And now she'd gone and got herself mixed up with a pair of brothers with territorial issues. Great.

Romy didn't share Clint's confidence about his

brother. Justin was a little too self-interested for her comfort, and his appreciation of the achievements of his staff was more to do with how that reflected on him. Still, she'd worked with his personality type before. The best strategy was to keep a safe distance and an open mind.

Maybe he was just struggling with younger-brother syndrome. Trying to prove himself to a complicated and unreachable man.

Romy laughed. Who knew they would have something in common!

Still…a little judicious internet surfing wouldn't go astray. A few subtle questions here and there. Just to put her niggling instincts to rest.

'Does your mum know you're here, Leighton?'

Unlikely, judging by the sheepish shrug of little shoulders. Clint groaned inwardly. As if he and Romy needed any more angst between them. It was going to be hard enough to work together without becoming an accomplice in her little boy's frequent misdemeanours. 'Come on, I'll walk home with you.'

Curious grey eyes so like his mothers stared at the tree house. 'Can't I come in?'

With the ghost of Romy still haunting his sanctuary, having Leighton in there was only going to double the uncomfortable rightness of it all. As though the house he thought he'd finished building a year ago was still waiting for the delivery of two finishing touches.

A wife.

A child.

Crazy thoughts when he'd built the tree house specifically to be a refuge for one. But hadn't he wondered as he built it what it would be like growing up here? The kind of person it would help make someone into? And hadn't he allowed his eyes to drift shut more than once and imagine a woman's arms snaking around his neck as he sat out on the balcony of an evening? A faceless, nameless woman, more of an essence than anything.

He had.

He swallowed. 'Maybe some other time. With your mother.'

Leighton groaned.

'Are you still mad at her from the other night?' Clint asked.

'She's mad at me. She's always mad at me.'

He was yet to see Romy angry at him in any way other than justified. He got the sense that this little kid was a minimaster in manipulation. And his mother was too frightened of losing him to take a risk. 'How does that make you feel?'

Leighton frowned. 'Mad.'

Clint's laugh coaxed a small one out of Leighton. It was hard not to enjoy this kid, his raw honesty. So like his mother. If he had a son he'd like him to be—

Whoa. Not going there. That stuff was best kept locked up tight in a secure place.

They walked on in companionable silence. 'How

was your hangout the other night?' He remembered at the very last second not to call it a sleepover.

'Cool!' Leighton launched into a blow-by-blow description of everything they did, activities and stories in which Steve Lawson featured quite highly. It got them three-quarters of the mile home. Finally, the story started to wind up.

'Sounds like a real boys' night,' Clint broke in on one of the rare occasions Leighton stopped for a breath.

'Cam's dad is so cool. He's a copper—I saw his gun.'

Clint frowned at the little eyes looking up at him so expectantly. 'You saw his weapon? In the house?'

'Uh-huh.'

There'd be no more hangouts at the Lawsons' if that was true. He stopped in his tracks and narrowed his eyes, pinning the eight-year-old hard, giving him the interrogatory stare he reserved for recalcitrant newbies in the unit. 'Really?'

Leighton couldn't hold it. His eyes flicked away. 'His holster, anyway. Where the gun would be.'

Okay. Not having to break that news to his mother was a massive relief. He wasn't confident that Romy wouldn't hold the messenger personally responsible.

'Yeah, Mr Lawson is way cool!' Then, as though Clint's feelings might be hurt, he hurried on, 'Oh, not as cool as you, though.'

Clint smiled. His feelings *were* a tiny bit dented. Hero-worship from the crowds at the flaming star awards ceremony had just felt insanely wrong. He'd felt a fraud. But from this little guy…it felt good. He didn't want to think that Leighton handed that out to just anyone.

Oh, get a grip. 'Police officers and soldiers have a bit in common.'

'Really?'

'Yep. Both charged with protecting the community, both highly trained, both taught to respect the uniform they wear and what it represents.'

'I'm going to be a soldier.'

Oh, your mother's not going to like that. 'Why not a police officer?'

'Or, yeah, a police officer.' Little grey eyes shot wide with sudden realisation. 'Ooh! Or a fireman!'

Getting warmer…

'What about a wildlife ranger? They have to protect the forest and they wear a uniform and have special training.' *And you'd make your mother the happiest woman on the whole planet.*

He seemed to consider it seriously and then his eyes grew more distant, hesitant. 'My granddad was a soldier. A big one.'

Back to the soldier thing. And knowing what little he did about Romy's relationship with her father, Leighton's slip-up was not good news. 'How do you know that? I thought you didn't know your grandfather?'

Leighton slowed his steps and looked away. Clint

could practically see the lie starting to take shape on his lips. 'The truth, champ.'

He looked balefully at Clint. 'He used to come and see me sometimes, at school. In the lunch break.'

Clint's whole body tightened up. What the hell was his school doing letting that happen? And what the hell was a man like Colonel Martin Carvell doing sneaking around a primary school?

He kept his voice carefully neutral. 'Does your mother know about that?'

The cautious stare turned angry. 'Are you going to tell her?'

Clint considered him as they approached the house. How did Romy negotiate this minefield every day? This precarious balancing act called parenting. Where every word counted. 'Nope. But might be a good idea if one day you do, just so she knows. You two shouldn't have any secrets between you.'

'You have secrets.'

Ah, there was that delightful eight-year-old petulance rearing its head. Clint frowned. 'Like what?'

'I heard Mum saying you were *full* of secrets.'

He couldn't imagine her chatting freely to just anyone about him, but his gut tightened up on instinct. 'Who was she talking with?'

'No-one. She was doing the vacuuming and getting angry.'

He had no trouble at all picturing that. So, Romy Carvell liked to beat on him while vacuuming? He smiled. That wasn't bad news. Not at all.

He liked that he affected her.

'Leighton! Again?' Romy's frustrated wail met them from across the clearing as she stomped down the house steps. Her focus wasn't even on Clint, but his body reacted instantly to the sight of her even at a distance. Remembering how she'd felt. How she'd smelt. How she'd almost tasted.

The hungry predator in him sniffed the air and salivated.

'See...' Leighton muttered, watching the steam train approaching.

Clint cleared his throat. 'You've brought this one on yourself, kiddo. You know you're not supposed to come to my place but you did it, anyway. You're going to have to take the consequences like a man.'

Leighton stared at him, but instead of turning on the pout, Clint saw something shift in his eyes and it translated in his body, in the way he pushed his shoulders back and faced his mother.

Faced his punishment.

Only there was none. Romy looked severe for just a moment before slipping her arms around her son's shoulders and pulling him close. Then she gave him a gentle shove towards the house. He ran off, every bit the child again. Entirely off the hook.

Clint sighed. *Baby steps.* Today was a start. For both of them.

He steeled himself against the woman in front of him.

Her hands went up. 'Don't start.'

'With what?'

'I'll be talking to him later about going off without permission. I didn't think this was the time or place.'

He burned to say something about the value of immediate reinforcement but he let it go. He had no right to tell her how to parent. Less than no right. He could clearly see how hard it was for her to discipline Leighton. He was like her Achilles heel. Besides, her full lips were dominating his focus right now. They were moving, and the pink of her tongue peeked in and out tantalisingly. And then they were pressing together. *Oh…*

'Sorry, what were you saying?' His voice was more gravelly than he would have liked. One kiss—not even that—and he was losing all composure. He had to pull it together.

She flushed, and he wondered whether she'd read his thoughts. Or maybe his expression. Well, it wasn't him that had run away from their encounter the other night. He'd been completely onboard with it.

Then.

Now, it just seemed a patently bad idea.

'I guess I'll see you at work sometime,' she repeated.

Sometime. That was code for 'not any time soon, thanks.' Well… If not for getting Leighton home just now, he'd be in the middle of giving Romy all the space she needed. And then some. Getting his life back on track. Back to how he liked it.

Quiet. Predictable. Everything within his control.

He didn't want Romy and her subtle lavender scent lingering in his consciousness any more than he wanted it lingering in his house. As if he could control either of those things. That made his choice easy.

'Maybe not. I've got some work to do around the tree house. I probably won't be getting down to the admissions area much.'

At all. It couldn't be disappointment staining her cheeks. She wanted him far away and he was taking care of that. She should be happy.

'Oh, okay. Well, then… I'll see you round, Clint.'

Not if he saw her first. All it took was that hint of gentle confusion in her eyes and the wild thing in him was clawing to be released. Until he could guarantee his stomach wouldn't lurch when he smelled her and his eyes wouldn't stray to her when she walked by…

The best defence was absence.

Until he could get complete control of his faculties when she was around. And if that was never…well, then…

He'd work out how to deal with that.

How could she have forgotten what Clint looked like filling a doorway? In only a week?

He braced himself with casual arms on top of the doorframe to the office kitchenette, the stretch pulling his muscles into intriguing angles. If not for the simmering storm in his eyes, Romy's heart might have lurched for very different reasons.

He was clean-shaven today. And that shirt looked new. He still seemed terrifying.

Beside her, Simone's jaw dropped in a most unlady-like fashion and her coffee mug tilted perilously close to losing its contents. But when he finally dragged his glare from Romy to her, Simone ditched the mug and turned to make a rapid excuse.

'I… Um…' Nothing came. 'Okay, 'bye.'

Clint stepped aside to let her flee and then filled the gap again, effectively cutting off any further escape.

Romy shook her head. She'd been just seconds away from ferreting out the information she needed about where Justin had worked in the US. 'You really don't try with people, do you, Clint?'

He prowled in through the door and leaned against the bench, his arms folded across his chest. 'Good morning to you, too.'

She matched his pose. Minus the casual lean. Her smile was tight, her sarcasm honed. 'Good morning, Clint. What can I do for you?' It wasn't as if he was in the neighbourhood. He'd tracked her down for a reason.

Dark eyes pinned her. 'How are you?'

They were not seriously going to do this? 'I'm fine. And you?'

He looked out at her from under very *non*-army-issue lashes. 'Okay, let's start again.' He nudged the kitchen door shut with his size-eleven boot and shifted closer to her. She shuffled back a little. Straight into the cabinetry. 'I'm sorry about what happened at my house. I didn't mean for it to…go that way.'

She read sincerity in his expression. Her shoulders loosened. 'I meant what I said. I can't afford to… I can't see past…some things. But it's not personal. I don't hold it against you.'

'That's good.'

It was in the change of light in his eyes—from an intense glowing to a loaded gleaming. She narrowed hers. 'Why is that good?'

'Because I was hoping… What are you doing Friday night?'

Her eyebrows shot up. Had all that solitude affected his brain? Surely she wasn't going to have to say it again?

He pushed on. 'The Hohloch Foundation is having a fundraiser in town. It's part of the million-acres habitat-protection program and all the major landowners in the region are expected to go.' His swallowed nervously. 'I'd like you to come along. Meet some of the locals. It's a good opportunity to network.'

There was a strange kind of vulnerability about him. 'So this is a work thing?'

'If that gets you there, yes,' he said. 'But you'll need a dress.'

The empathy evaporated completely. She pressed her lips together. 'You say that like I might not have one!'

'I mean a dance dress. A gown. It's formal.'

Her arms crossed protectively in front of her. 'Just

because you've never seen me in a dress doesn't mean I don't own one! Every woman has a formal dress.'

He raised two hands. 'Ceasefire, cadet. I just wanted to make sure you understood what kind of a gig it was.'

She knew what *fundraiser* meant. How many kinds of idiot did he think she was? 'You think I might embarrass WildSprings? Turn up in my underwear?'

His green eyes flared.

'You're the hermit, McLeish. I'd be more worried about what you'll be wearing.'

He ignored that. 'So you'll come?'

'If it's a work thing, yes. I'll be there. *In a dress.*'

He straightened and turned to release the door. 'Great. I'll pick you up at six.'

'Wait! Why do I need a lift?'

He looked at her, quizzically. 'We're neighbours going to the same event, sixty clicks away. You think we should drive separately?'

Nice one, Carvell. Way to appear more competent in his eyes. *Think, think.* She had to wrestle back some control. 'Um, I could collect you?'

He stared her down. 'You want to pick me up?'

No. She lifted her chin. 'Yes. It seems only fair.'

He smiled and shrugged. 'Fine. I'll be waiting for you at six.'

Romy fumed as he walked out of the kitchenette. Damn him! Finding her, cornering her in the kitchen, insulting her wardrobe. And her professionalism. Her chest heaved with unvented passion. Then her indignation started to settle as the reality set in. Sixty kilometres there, a full night out and then sixty home. Together. Alone. With the man she'd been unable to get her mind off but couldn't be in the same room as.

And—brilliant!—she was driving him so she couldn't leave early with one of the other staff. She roared her frustration as she tossed her half-drunk coffee into the sink. *Damn!* She'd just been played by an expert.

And—*damn!*—she'd have to buy a dress.

Oh, Lord…

Romy saw him the moment she pulled up at the base of the tree house sharp on six o'clock. He looked like a model striding towards her on a catwalk made of beams from her headlights.

She swallowed. He'd cut his hair short. Not quite military enough to make her nervous but close enough to highlight the square line of his jaw and to reveal the smooth arc of a forehead that served as a canvas for his fringed, sage eyes.

How on earth had he ever found a coat to fit those shoulders? It wasn't a tuxedo, but the expensive black fabric draped on him like a second skin. Black suit, black shirt, black tie. She suddenly got a flash of what he must have looked like in full Taipan ops gear. He would have carried himself and fifty kilos of equipment with the same easy grace as he sauntered towards her now.

You will not find that sexy…

Her little pep talk helped for a moment. But only a moment. Clint stopped in front of the car and stared at her. All her usual Romy-isms failed her. No single eyebrow lift, no sarcastic comment, no impatient sigh. Her eyes struggled to free themselves from the compelling hold of his.

The blood pumping through her heart ached.

Then that beautiful mouth twisted in the glow of light and he held up a perfectly manicured hand and folded all four fingers towards him, just once. His sights remained locked on her.

Don't get out.

Her driver assist started dinging as the door sprung open and she swung her Manolo Blahniks out onto the leafy earth. As she pulled herself to her feet, the silken sheath of her dress slithered back down to her calves, cool and sensual against her skin.

Clint squinted in the headlights as she stepped out from behind the driver's door. It was like approaching a wild animal; moving towards him was not an option, so she circled him carefully, not taking her focus off him lest he lunge. He followed her every step, focus still fixed on her, until she joined him in the headlights.

His Adam's apple worked overtime lurching upwards from the black tie that constrained it. Heat seemed to radiate off him, even in the relative cool of evening.

Her spirit finally battled her way through the seductive fog enveloping her. She lifted one brow in question.

He shook his head. 'You look…amazing.' His voice could have melted ice.

She felt amazing. Doubly so as she saw herself reflected in the dark pools of his eyes. Her embroidered bodice followed the contours of her bust snugly, giving her a boost in all the right places. Her confidence not the least. Then it draped over her waist and hips and fell in luxurious fawn folds to her ankles. Green eyes grazed leisurely up the length of her.

Her pulse thrummed in places she'd never guessed she had one. 'You look…dangerous. But good.' How could it feel as though he was touching her when they were a metre apart? So much for keeping a safe distance.

'I'm feeling a bit dangerous right now,' he said. 'Maybe we should get going?'

She turned back to the car but his large hand came out and wrapped around hers. Around the keys clenched nervously in it.

'I'd like to drive,' he said. 'And before you protest… no, this is not a guy thing. I just… Cinderella should not have to drive herself to the ball.'

Oh. She swallowed past the sudden knot in her throat. His fingers were warm and steady around hers as he stepped closer. Even in three-inch heels she still had to tip her head to look at him.

'Will you let me drive, Romy?'

He said *drive* like he meant *make love to you*. In a

voice of pure molten lava. Her body trembled. No way was she capable of arguing.

Stop it!

She stepped back and released the clutch of keys to him, working hard not to simply stumble around to the passenger side. Unaccustomed as she was to serious heels, and with barely any courage left in her legs, it wasn't easy. She sank gratefully into the leather seat and then arranged her feet and skirt modestly in front of her, smoothing nervous hands down her thighs a few times. The repetition was comforting.

Excellent. Her obsessive compulsive disorder was coming along nicely....

'You're going to have to stop that, or I'll drive us off the road.'

Startled eyes shot up to meet dark ones and her hands froze. Clint's focus dropped to where she'd smoothed the fabric tightly against her thighs as his capable, tanned hands turned the ignition. Heat blazed through the car and not all of it was coming from him.

Sixty kilometres.

Oh, my...

CHAPTER SEVEN

THE one thing Romy had not expected this evening was to have a good time.

She'd nearly tumbled from the car on arrival, desperate to escape the intense chemistry saturating her little Honda for the past thirty minutes. Sixty kilometres was not far by country standards but she'd never taken a longer journey in her life.

They'd made polite small talk—in the car and throughout the evening so far—while ignoring the rampant hormones swirling around them like an aura. The *thing* between them was not getting any less, particularly not while they were both dressed to undress.

Arriving and melting into the throng of other similarly clad partiers helped to dilute her intense awareness of what she wore and how it affected Clint. And how him being affected was affecting her. But despite all the suits in the beautifully done up venue and all the strapping, country men wearing them, there was not a man here who so much as touched the presence Clint McLeish commanded.

Eyes followed him wherever he went. Curious ones, ambitious ones, envious ones. And one particularly grey, particularly conflicted pair that sought him out against her will, even now, and divided their time equally between his hands and his lips.

Romy tore her attention back to the room in general. Half the district was here and she recognised a few faces. Simone, in the corner having an animated conversation full of wild gesticulations that tossed splashes of white wine everywhere. Justin, by the bar, looking bored. She nodded and raised her drink to Carolyn and Steve Lawson, who'd been gracious enough to add Leighton to their brood having a popcorn and movie night, watched over by a child-minder. They started towards her with welcome smiles on their faces but then Carolyn suddenly reached out and halted Steve's progress, dragging him off in another direction entirely.

'Care for a refill?' Clint appeared next to her, a glass of champagne in one hand and what looked like juice in the other.

She caught open speculation and amusement in Carolyn's expression a moment before her friend disappeared into the crowd.

'No, thank you. I've had my one. Driving, remember?'

Clint graciously handed her the juice and then dropped the untouched champagne onto the tray of a passing waiter. She looked at him curiously.

'You won't have it?' She hadn't seen him with

alcohol in his hand all night. She frowned again. Ever, in fact.

He surveyed the room, absently. 'I don't drink.'

That didn't surprise her. She'd never met a better candidate for alcoholism.

As if he read her mind, he elaborated. 'I don't like to blur my faculties. In my line of business that's counterproductive.'

She didn't miss his use of the present tense. 'To running a posh retreat in the country?'

He dropped his gaze back to hers, his smile tight. 'With you I need to stay on my toes.' His gaze swept over her embroidered bodice so quickly she thought she'd imagined it. 'My senses are already addled enough without adding liquor to the equation.'

The heat in his eyes told her exactly what—who— was responsible for that. *Addled* was a good word for how she'd been feeling all night herself. She blinked up at him.

'What are we doing?' she squeaked as she suddenly found herself being towed towards the dance floor.

'It's called dancing, Romy. People like it.' His voice thinned.

'You didn't ask me if I wanted to dance!' Okay, now she really was just picking a fight.

'I didn't need to. You look like you either want to be kissed or touched. Given the gathered audience, I'm going for touched.'

Her mouth gaped like the trout Clint stocked in WildSprings's waterways. He swung her into a tiny gap on the crowded dance floor, forcing them to press close together. Extremely close together. Her body still fit perfectly against his. Her heels meant her cheek was closer to his shoulder than his chest, for a change, but otherwise the hardness of his body and the softness of hers merged as they effortlessly moved to the gentle music.

This is not heavenly, this is not heavenly…

But, oh, Lord, it was pure heaven. She didn't have enough experience with men to know whether all dancing felt like this. Whether all men smelled like he did. Whether all kisses tingled like his had. Every living part of her wanted to crawl into the circle of his arms and never come out. To be cherished and spoiled and watched over forever. To be able to put aside the load…just for a little bit.

It was almost as seductive as the feel of his hips pressed close against hers by the crowd. And they were only dancing. Imagine how it would be if—

'No!' She pulled away from him. Tense heat simmered down on her but he gave her some air. If not complete freedom. She trained her focus where his hands still held her in a velvet vice.

'I didn't realise agreeing to come along tonight meant I'd be chained to your side all evening.' Okay, it was a bitch of a thing to say but she had to put some space between them. And if it couldn't be physical…

His nostrils flared, his eyes blazed, but he remained silent. And his hold on her loosened a hint further. But not entirely. She scanned the room nervously, hoping for salvation. It wasn't that she was in any danger, but she suddenly didn't feel…safe.

His face tightened. 'You're going to have to do something about the mixed messages you're sending, Romy. They're triggering my innate need to conquer. I'm trained to overcome obstacles and you do have a way of stacking them up irresistibly.'

Conquer. Overcome. These were not concepts she was comfortable with but they roused some slumbering beast living deep inside of her. A creature that didn't crack open an eye very often. A fundamental, ancient need to align herself with the strongest male, one who could provide and protect.

And procreate.

The most base level of survival instincts. And Romy was struggling with the purely chemical, Darwinian response of a mammal recognising its perfect mate.

She stumbled in his hold.

'Romy, would you like to dance?' Steve Lawson was suddenly by her side, materialising out of nowhere. His ruddy cheeks were paler than usual but he had a determined expression on his face and, after only a moment of doubt, he met Clint's less-than-pleased glare. 'You don't mind, mate, right?'

Oh, bless you and your country courage, Steven Lawson! Knights in shining armour sometimes didn't come on a horse. Carolyn's anxious face bobbed in and out of view across the crowded room. Romy freed herself from the strong grip keeping her captive.

'Thank you, Steve, I'd love to. And, no, he doesn't mind.'

She practically fell into her friend's careful hold as Clint dissolved back into the crowd. For the first minute, Steve did all the work, holding her upright, keeping her moving, chatting away casually, and it gave her the time she needed to recover her composure.

Somewhat.

When the dance ended, someone else swooped in to take Steve's place. A complete and welcome stranger. Then another and another. Romy danced with half the town before she began to suspect Carolyn was orchestrating this social interference. Either that or the novelty of a single woman willing to dance in a female-deficient environment had caught on. Regardless, the result was the same. After one unsuccessful attempt to reclaim her, Clint had taken up post in the corner of the room, scaring off with a glare anyone who approached him.

Not that she was watching.

She was exhausted when the band finally stopped for a break, but—amazingly—she really had enjoyed being the belle of the ball. When else in her life had that ever happened? She'd met a swag of new people and, conveniently, it gave her the perfect excuse not to think about the giant thundercloud in the corner.

Or her feelings for him, more specifically.

Her pleasure at the flattering attentions of the men in the room was not a patch on the intense rush she'd experienced when Clint had first seen her this evening.

He'd called her Cinderella and, standing in the glow of her Honda's headlights clothed in a fairytale dress and shoes costing a fortnight's salary, it was exactly how she'd felt. Like no rules applied tonight because it was a magical night.

And Clint had been her prince. His frank appraisal in the headlights had been both honest and raw. The liquid magma heating his gaze had come from a place so deep she found it impossible not to respond.

But then they'd made small talk. Danced. Argued. And the real world came crashing back in the same split second she realised she was badly attracted to Clint McLeish. Biologically attracted. Damaged, angry, *military* Clint. A man torn apart from the institution which sustained him—that he still very clearly wished he was a part of. A man trained in the same methodology as her father.

She reached for the table edge to steady herself.

What kind of cosmic reward was this? She'd done her best to overcome challenges in life, had never once complained about the predicament her own foolish actions had left her in. She'd studied and worked hard and had taken on a grown-up's responsibility before she really was one. And her reward…?

To find herself perilously close to falling for the absolute worst kind of man for her.

She closed her eyes and took several deep, steadying breaths.

'Romy?'

She spun around, blinking, her internal radar going into alarm. 'Oh, Justin. Hi.'

His eyes narrowed, as though he heard the disappointment in her voice. 'You've danced with everyone but me this evening.'

No more dancing. Not now. All she really wanted to do was go home. 'Justin, I'm sorry. I'm all tuckered out.'

He frowned. 'I'm serious, Romy. Every man here. Except me.'

She matched his expression, smelled the alcohol on him. 'I understand, Justin. But I'm sorry, I'm tired.'

Justin slipped both arms around her waist and pulled her into a close embrace. 'Dance with me....'

This close, his eyes were like his brother's. But where Clint's slumbered with sensuality, Justin's swilled with liquor and raw, hard sexual interest. What was he doing? Justin only ever spoke to her on the strictest business terms—was the whole damned world upside down tonight? She pushed ineffectually against him, trying to break free. He resisted. So she did the next best thing, slipped her hands up his back and found the magic spot in his left shoulder...and pressed with all her strength.

Justin staggered to the side, his left arm dropping away uselessly. 'Son of a...'

'I said no, Justin. Perhaps you didn't hear me?' Icicles could have formed on her words. A few nearby faces turned towards them.

He glared at her, embarrassed and more than a little ashamed, judging by his colour. 'It was just a dance.'

It was just the liquor. Her mind took her immediately to another man, one who eschewed the addling effects of alcohol. She sought him out across the room but his corner was empty. She turned back to Justin, a hollow feeling in her chest.

'Does it still hurt?' She knew from her martial-arts training it wouldn't. It was a pressure-point trick. Like pinching the funny bone. But less funny.

He rubbed at the offending shoulder, avoiding eye contact. 'No, it's fine. I apologise. I think I've had too much to drink.'

You think? He was still her boss, technically. Romy erred on the side of caution. 'Don't worry about it, Justin. Maybe you need some air?'

He mumbled something and wandered off in the direction of the bar. Romy sighed and scooped her clutch purse from the table. Perhaps she could sit in the car until the formalities were over. She slid out of a side door and walked down the side of the building to the parking area at the rear.

Out of nowhere, steel hands closed around her waist and pulled her near off her feet into the shadows of a doorway.

'Clint!'

'If you've quite finished playing up to every man here?' he grated.

It was a little bit too close to an echo from her past. *Whore.* She pushed against him wholeheartedly and got exactly nowhere. She glared. 'It's called dancing, Clint. People like it.'

His eyes smouldered in the moonlight. 'Lord save me from smart-mouthed women.'

His gaze fell to her mouth the instant he uttered the word. Her breath puffed angrily out of it as she wrestled to be free. But she felt the touch of his look as truly as if it had been his lips on hers.

'And smart-brained women. Can you not let me have one single point?'

She stopped wriggling and met the iron in his gaze. If she gave an inch now she'd give him everything. 'No.'

It was too close. Much too close to the moment she discovered she wanted a man that she could never have. She couldn't be pressed against him like this and not want more. And she did. So much more.

'Why are you out here?' she asked as he let her step away.

He shrugged. 'I got tired of watching the Romy Carvell show.'

Slap. That hurt. The single time she got to be the princess for a night and he found a way of making it sound selfish. She turned out of the shadows, wrenching free on a sucked-in breath.

'Romy, wait.' Gentle pressure manacled her wrist, pulled her back into the doorway. 'I couldn't… I'm not a good mixer, like you. I struggle with people.' His lids dropped like shutters over vulnerable eyes.

Struggle with people. That was the understatement of all time.

'This is the first time I've really been out. In this kind of setting since…' He dug his hands into his pockets. 'I needed the backup.'

Romy blinked. Surely not? 'What about the city?'

He looked up, bemused. 'What about it?'

'Well, don't you… There'd be lots of places just like this. When you go there?'

He regarded her steadily. 'What do you think I do when I'm in the city?'

Suddenly she sounded like Simone. Passing on idle gossip. 'Um…'

His eyes flared briefly. 'I see. You think I dig myself out of deepest isolation in the forest and then hit the clubs cruising for sex. Is that about right?'

There was no undoing what she'd implied, but she couldn't bring herself to say yes aloud. But she had to say something. 'What do you go for?'

The muffled sound of the band filled the silence stretching between them. His lashes dropped again. He shook his head, slightly. 'Not that.'

Oh.

He took a deep breath, lifted his face to meet her gaze. 'I only came tonight because you were here. I was relying on you to…'

She tilted her head. 'To…?'

'I hoped you'd be my buffer. Help me transition.'

Romy frowned. She'd left him in a room full of strangers while she danced the night away. Guilt tore through her but her subconscious fought it. She spoke gently. 'This wasn't a date, Clint.'

He straightened. 'I'm not making excuses, just explaining why I'm out here. Why I'm staying here.'

The realisation hit her. This was too hard for him. Big, bad, grumpy Clint McLeish was out of his depth. At a small-town fundraiser. That was why he stood alone in the corner not talking to anyone. It had nothing to do with being elitist.

He could parachute into dangerous foreign territory but he couldn't stomach a single night amongst strangers. Her heart softened.

She peered up at him. 'Do you want to go home?'

His lids fluttered down for the barest of moments, and when they opened, naked flame flickered behind them. 'You think of WildSprings as home?'

She blushed. 'Your home.' Then she realised how that sounded and blushed harder. Metaphorical midnight had well and truly struck and the princess was reverting into plain old, foot-in-mouth Cinders by the second. 'We can go whenever you want.'

'I'm quite comfortable in here,' he said, settling closer against her.

She realised how small the doorway was they were sheltering in. If anyone should walk by…how would it look? She leaned back a little. 'You can't stand here alone all night.'

'I don't have to be alone.' Large hands reached out and snaked around her waist, stealing her breath and pulling her gently against him, hot and exciting where they touched. 'We never got to finish our dance.'

Walk away, Romy.

What had happened to the smart, savvy woman who'd raised a child, protected a family and sacrificed everything for her son? She fled completely in the face of the blatant desire pulsing from the oversize testosterone bomb in front of her.

A surge of want answered deep in her body. The primal creature hungering for satisfaction. How bad could it be to give Cinderella one last dance with the prince? Clint sensed her acquiescence and pulled her gently into his arms. She let herself lean into his solid frame, tucked in closer than she needed to be even in the close confines of the doorway, and pressed her cheek to his shoulder. He gathered her up against him. Their feet started moving in time with the distant music but it was automatic. Romy couldn't hear a thing over the march of his heart under her ear. It took only seconds for her own to fall into sync.

Thrum…thrum…thrum…

Her hands slipped around behind him, spread across his massive back, splayed and sure. He cocooned her until her face buried in the crook of his neck, comfortably, snugly. Like the safe harbour of her fantasies.

Nothing could harm her while she was in these arms.

They shuffled left and right, barely moving in the evening breeze. Seasons came and went, ages passed, continents drifted, and still they pressed together, swaying.

Clock's ticking, Cinders.

It felt entirely natural to tilt her face and nuzzle the place below Clint's jaw. To breathe in the scent of him. To press her mouth into the heavy, thumping pulse there. To taste smooth, male skin for the first time. Her lips roamed his throat, her breasts lifting and falling against his chest, and she pushed onto her toes so she could reach his ear to take one perfect lobe softly between her teeth. It took an eternity.

The rumble in her ears sounded like thunder, but it came from deep inside Clint. The primitive growl excited the blood in her veins as his hands slid up to pull her harder against his straining body. She pulled one hand free and shoved it roughly through his hair, anchoring herself there and using it to hoist herself upwards so she could feast on the heady taste of him. She sank into his throat like a vampire starving for blood.

'Romy...' It was more choke than word. Male and raw.

Her breasts strained against the bodice of her dress, almost coming entirely free as she stretched towards him. His hands found the bare, hot skin of her shoulders. The soft, sensitive flesh of her nape. The wild, flushed heat of her cheeks. They braced her jaw, tore her away from her decadent feeding and tilted her gaze upwards. She had just enough seconds to suck in a breath before those magnificent, sinful lips dropped decisively onto hers.

The heavens exploded into brilliant colours as his mouth touched hers for the first time. There was no gentle teasing, no careful initiation. Clint forced his way straight into the depths of her mouth, using only the power of his raw sexuality. She'd dreamed about those lips but even her most fever-inducing fantasies were nothing on the real deal. The actual taste and feel of his hot mouth crushing against hers. His powerful tongue thrusting in and out. His strong hands clenching in her hair.

He lifted her off her feet and spun around to press her into the wall, not leaving her lips for longer than it took to groan into the night and heave in a shuddering breath. His body alone pinned her against the bricks, leaving his hands free to roam wildly over her.

Up, down, up again. And all the while he plundered the depths of her mouth, dangerously hard and fantastically hot.

And utterly, utterly mind-blowing.

Romy moaned and pure sexual instinct made her hook her legs around his hips, securing her position, wanting to get closer. Anything to relieve the ache building deep at her core. She sank her fingers into the thick, short crop of his hair, panting heavily, and met his assault on her mouth.

He pushed the fabric of her dress hard up her legs and stroked the rounded flesh of her thighs and bottom.

Her sensitised skin screamed at the torture. She thrust her head back for air. He zeroed in on her throat.

'Whoa! People, get a room!'

Romy froze. Clint stiffened and dragged his mouth off her. In the same moment, they both seemed to realise what they were doing. And where. And with whom. The stranger wobbled away from them laughing, carrying a half-drunk beer and a spare one for later.

The bright explosion of light wasn't in her mind, Romy realised. It was real. The fireworks entertainment had started, bringing all the fundraiser guests out into the garden, only twenty metres from where she was half naked in a doorway with her legs wrapped around a Special Forces operative.

CHAPTER EIGHT

'LET me down.'

Her voice was tight and cold where moments ago it had been hot and wet against his lips, moaning against his ear.

Clint lowered her carefully to the ground, using his body to shield her from the view of any other drunken idiots who might wander by. He was in no condition to turn around, anyway, so giving Romy a moment to pull herself together was a win for both of them.

What the hell had he done?

Her chest heaved with her gasping breath, highlighting her perfect cleavage a treat from his height. The shadowed curves begged him to worship them. *That's* what he'd done. Let his hormones overrule his head. The thing he was trained never to do. Sex, alcohol, fear—none of which were supposed to affect his judgement or his precision.

Except it wasn't only hormones. His heart was getting involved now, and where in his many years of training did anyone say anything about hearts?

'I need to get out of here...'

Her face was pale, her hair and makeup dishevelled. No way could she go back in there tonight looking as if she'd been doing exactly what she had been. It was hard to tell what upset her more, getting hot and heavy with him…or being caught doing it.

'Romy—'

She thrust both hands in front of his face. 'Don't, Clint.'

He stepped away. Her shields came up faster than on the *Starship Enterprise*.

'I need a minute…' Her breathing was erratic.

She pressed past him and his stupid, starving body still leapt at her touch. It hadn't been that long surely? Did he have no resistance left whatsoever? Blinding flashes of colour went off above them. Each one painted her face a different shade of pale.

She started to stumble off. 'I'll meet you by the car.'

'I'll just go in and give our—' she was gone before he'd finished '—apologies.'

He closed his eyes and punched both fists against the wall on a curse. He'd really screwed up this time. As if sharing his difficulty around strangers wasn't stupid enough, he'd also pretty much mauled her in the back alley of a pub. Slammed her against the wall.

Nice. Real nice.

His straining body reminded him that he'd be buried deep inside her right now if they hadn't been interrupted. He'd be coaxing tiny sounds out of her beautiful throat. It's where they were heading. He was, anyway.

Galloping there. And not just because he had three years of abstinence at his heels. He shook his head and called himself every name under the Australian sun. It satisfactorily dowsed the surge in his trousers so he could walk inside, find their host and make apologies. Absolutely the last thing he wanted to do, but exactly the sort of thing Romy would do if she was able.

And so he did it for her.

It meant forcing himself into a room crowded with faces he didn't know, convinced he was marked with a giant *B* for bastard, and certain half the room knew what he'd just done to Romy Carvell out in the alley. Heat flamed under his choking tie.

He wasn't an idiot. He saw how the townsfolk rallied to keep her occupied on the dance floor. It meant they'd accepted her as one of their own and even taken her under their collective wing. In a way they never had with him. Even Steve Lawson had fronted him when things got a bit tense out there.

And given that Sergeant Lawson was one of very few people authorised to know what he did for a living before coming home to WildSprings, that took some fairly big *cojones* on Steve's part. But he'd done it for Romy. They all had.

What was it about her that had an entire town running interference? Trying to protect her.

Had *him* wanting to protect her…despite tonight's complete stuff-up.

* * *

Romy marched up and down the rows of cars neatly parked on the football field behind the pub, breathing deeply. Even a town like Quendanup and the surrounding districts could turn up a big crowd when it wanted to. The dazzling fireworks show went on overhead and insects crash-darted into her, blinded by their attraction to the floodlights that kept the forty vehicles securely lit.

She stared at a large, fuzzy moth that plopped, exhausted, onto the dusty bonnet of a Land Cruiser. It flipped uselessly on singed wings and then lay twitching in the breeze. Stupid things—they'd fly themselves quite literally to death before they'd learn not to orbit the dazzling floodlights.

Remind you of anyone?

She kicked back into gear and resumed her manic pacing.

Just. Stay. Away. How hard could that be on a property as big as WildSprings? What kind of masochistic moth was she to keep putting herself within burning distance of Clint's brilliant glow? He wasn't obvious and showy like the almost-day football lights. He was darker, closer to an ultraviolet black light—harmless to the naked eye but irresistible to hapless moths passing by.

And entirely deadly.

Thoughts tumbled, unordered, through her mind. Was it wrong to want to march right up there and climb back into his strong arms? To discover what their two bodies would have felt like coming together?

To give herself until midnight and only *then* face the real world?

Lord, it tempted her.

She'd been so disgustingly good her whole life. Restrained and reasonable and safe. The single blot on her copybook was that fateful night when the Colonel's bullying had finally driven her to brand her body and then give away her innocence to a stranger. Both of which, as it transpired, were completely irrevocable.

And now this. Letting herself get involved with the most inappropriate man possible. Damaged, reclusive, *military* goods. The third stupid thing she'd done in her life. But at least this she had a hope of walking away from.

'Ugh!'

Agony shot through her left foot as two inches of her three-inch Manolo sank to the side in the soft turf of the football field while the rest of her dropped like a stun-gun victim the other way. The delicate tangle of tendons and muscles in her ankle wrenched violently.

As if her night wasn't ruined as it was—now her beautiful dress would have grass stains. And not from anything worth getting grass stains for! She rolled onto her side to slip her foot out of the trapped stiletto, and then pulled herself up against the bumper of a nearby 4WD, drawing her foot to her body and pressing her hands around her damaged ankle. Shocked tears welled dangerously.

You're not seriously thinking about crying?

The Colonel's voice again. Romy sucked in a series of deep breaths and looked around urgently for something to focus on. Studying the minute details of objects—anything—had always helped her head off the tears her father wouldn't tolerate.

Light from the fireworks bounced in a beautiful spectrum off the broken headlight of the vehicle she was half hanging onto. Her arm looped around the roo bar and she pulled herself into a more upright position, ignoring the sharp stab in her leg. Any second now it would be a nasty throb and then a horrible ache.

She stared at the way the light fragmented and bounced off the many facets of the shattered headlight, depending on where she moved her head. Amazing how light worked. It really was very pretty. The wash in her eyes trebled the effect. She swiped at them with her free arm while hoisting herself further up into a sitting position on using the heavy 4WD for ballast. Sure enough, the tears eventually subsided.

Thanks for something, Colonel.

Romy reached down and slipped her remaining shoe off and tossed it over to its offending partner. Her ankle didn't so much scream as moan.

Twisted, then, not broken.

As she prepared to pull herself up onto her good foot, the final fireworks of the evening went off with a loud crack. Thousands of bright embers showered earthwards like a supersize sparkling jellyfish, falling harmlessly to the ground and throwing a daylight-bright glow onto everything around her. One tire of the 4WD was right next to her face and the fireworks lit it perfectly. Romy stared, knowing exactly where she'd seen that distinctive tread before.

On a seldom-used track at WildSprings.

She shoved away from the roo bar in disgust and scrambled over to her shoes, ignoring the sharp protest of her injured ankle and knowing this was the same view that kangaroo would have taken to its grave. From below, the vehicle was all wheels, chrome and bug-encrusted grille. The tread marks at the scene had been so distinctive. There couldn't possibly be two of them in the same district.

She scrabbled for her clutch purse, pulled out her mobile phone and called up the photo from the roo-strike site. It matched these tyres perfectly. She snapped a new one, this time of the tire itself, a second and third of the vehicle emblem and the broken head-light and finally the registration plate on the 4WD.

How she'd love to get her hands on whoever was driving roughshod through her park.

Her park? Ooh, that felt way too good on the lips.

She shoved her phone back into her clutch and started to push herself up, trying to right her legs from their awkward, splayed position. Like an obscene Barbie doll someone had tossed to the ground with its glamorous outfit all hiked high.

'Romy, what the hell have you done?' Clint appeared from nowhere and scooped her into a standing position, taking most of her weight. She tugged at her dress, desperate to restore some dignity. *But, really, what was the point?*

She opened her mouth, about to tell him about the 4WD and its tyres.

'Seriously, can I not leave you alone for five minutes?' he muttered, shaking his head.

She stiffened in his hold and her chest tightened up. Now *that* was classic Colonel. Would Clint never see her as anything other than an amusement to be humoured, comforted or rescued? Even after running his hands all over her in the alley?

He bent to lift her into his arms. All thought of the 4WD fled. 'What are you doing?' she cried, lurching away from him, balancing on one leg and counter-balancing with her clutch and her shoes in the other hand.

His handsome face frowned. 'I'm going to carry you to the car.'

'Like hell you are! I can get there myself.'

'Really?' He straightened and glared at her, all hints of desire gone. He glanced down where she held her damaged foot carefully off the ground. 'Fine, knock yourself out.'

With my luck I probably will.

She braced her shoe hand on the bonnet of the 4WD and used it as a crutch, pitching away a metre. She regained her balance and then pushed herself forwards until she hit the front of the next car in line.

'Romy, let me help. Please.' He growled right behind her. 'I'll just pick you up.'

'No.' Her concentration frown was so intense it almost marred her view and she braced herself on the bonnet and then pushed off on her good foot.

This might actually work.

'Then let me be your crutch...'

'You're too tall.' She lunged towards the next car in the row and nearly missed, catching herself on the bad ankle. She wasn't quick enough to swallow the cry.

'For God's sake, let me carry you.' He was right there, hovering.

She couldn't touch him again. Not without crying. 'Clint, no! I need to do this by myself.'

Need to? Where had that come from? Damn.

He backed off—just a little—and let her go, shadowing close behind. It was excruciating in pain and speed but she would have dragged herself home with her fingernails to get her point across.

She was a capable woman. He needed to see her as one.

About halfway to her car she remembered the 4WD, and roughly three-quarters of the way there she decided not to tell him about it. She wanted to solve it first. Come to him with a resolution, not a problem. She had contacts in the police department who could run those plates on the quiet. Give her an idea of who was yahooing in the park.

She lurched onwards.

Finally, she reached her Honda, practically gasping with exhaustion. Clint stepped around in front of her, took one look at the unshed tears in her eyes and his lips thinned impossibly further. But his voice dropped down a measure.

'Have you quite finished with the Xena: Warrior Princess act?'

She dashed at her lashes. 'If you hadn't been here I would have had to get myself to the car. Why would I do any different just because you are?' *Just because I'm dying for you to hold me.*

His frown doubled. 'If I wasn't here, you wouldn't have been aerating the pitch with your heels in the first place.'

True enough. Romy collapsed onto the passenger seat and swung her good leg in, then carefully lifted her damaged one beside it. 'Do you mind driving?'

His expression answered for him. He crossed around to the front of the car and then slid in behind the wheel. The interior light faded as soon as his door closed and he turned the key she passed him too hard, double-jacking the motor.

She stiffened in her seat. She and anger didn't play well. She'd spent a lifetime trying to avoid conflict with her father; she didn't need it in her new life in the country. Sitting right beside her.

But it looked like conflict had found her.

They drove out of town in complete silence, not even the radio to provide some light relief. Simply breathing felt like wading through congealed molasses. She fixed her stare out into the inky darkness, trying to ignore Clint's tangible simmer.

Failing.

Angry-Romy was all tuckered out. Being mad was too much work. Reasonable-Romy hopped from foot to foot in the wings, waiting for her chance to get a word in.

It came.

Running away from him without a word had been rude. She'd kissed him willingly. He hadn't forced her to spear her hands through his hair or press her mouth to his throat. Those were her decisions. And she'd run because of the whole military thing—

Liar.

The little voice shocked a gasp out of her. Clint glanced sideways at her briefly through the darkened cabin, then tracked his attention back onto the road ahead.

Tell the truth, girl.

The Colonel. Relentless about honesty and personal responsibility. She frowned into the night. It *was* the truth! Wasn't it? She took herself back to that darkened doorway, relived the feelings. Clint's power, his confidence. The broad, hard contours of his shoulders. The short, sexy spikes of his newly cut hair. The way he'd shielded her with his body from prying eyes. She'd responded to all the parts of him that were classic military.

Her eyes rounded in the reflection of the side window as she realised. She hadn't run from that part of him, she'd run *towards* it. Even in heels. The capable, military part of him was attractive to her on a primeval, fundamental level.

She blew out a confused breath. 'The last time I had sex I got pregnant.'

Amazing, really, that he didn't drive clear off the road. But his voice was tight when he finally spoke. 'Excuse me?'

Romy took a deep breath. 'It was also the first time I had sex. Which would pretty much make it the only time I've had sex.' Oh, for crying out loud, she couldn't even stop *saying* 'sex' around him.

He glanced over at her, confused. 'You've had one sexual encounter in your life and you got pregnant out of it?'

She shrugged her shoulders, too casually. 'I'm the reason young girls are warned about the first time, I guess.'

He glanced between the road and her. Twice. On a curse, he slammed the brakes and pulled off into a lay-by, cutting the motor and staring at her in the darkened car.

She returned the stare. Then she couldn't stand it any longer. 'For two years it was all about surviving my father, protecting my baby. After that I had a toddler to raise and food to scrounge together. By the time Leighton was at school I'd kind of…gone off the whole…romance thing.'

He shook his head. 'Just once?'

Romy balled her fists. He really wasn't getting her. 'Can we move past the slack-jawed shock, do you think?'

'You're practically a virgin.'

Okay, so maybe he was on the same page. She cleared her throat. 'I...really don't count that first time at all. So...yes.'

'Why doesn't it count?'

'I was—' Half in shock? Violently drunk? Present-absent? '—not really involved.'

Clint's eyes focused on her.

'Were you forced?'

She shook her head, flushing. 'I wanted to rebel against my father. The guy was just my weapon of choice. But I also chose not to actively...participate... in the end.' She couldn't. It was why she was twenty-six and had never been properly kissed. Let alone loved. 'Obviously I didn't plan to...didn't realise I'd get pregnant.'

A high-pitched creaking sound filled the little Honda. Romy realised it was Clint's hands squeezing the life out of her leather steering-wheel cover. He muttered an obscenity under his breath.

Her defences shot up instantly. 'Don't judge me, Clint.'

Wow. Thinking it and saying it were two very different things. There was a kind of power in actually verbalising the words.

Don't. Judge. Me.

His eyes zeroed back in on hers. 'Judging you? You're practically a virgin, Romy, and I was about to take you up against a wall in an alleyway. How do you think that makes me feel?'

She lifted her voice to match his. 'Don't judge

yourself either. I just wanted you to understand why I took off like that. It was rude and I'm sorry.'

Words failed him. Then he laughed, strained and thin. 'You don't sound sorry—you sound really ticked off.'

'If you keep pushing me I will get ticked off.' Lord, it was amazing to speak her mind! 'I simply wanted you to know why I left.'

'I assumed it was the military thing.'

She stared at him, breathing heavily. 'So did I, at first.'

'But not now?'

Her voice dropped to a bare whisper. 'It still bothers me, Clint. I would be lying if I said it didn't. But I recognise that it's a big part of you.'

Wordless seconds ticked by. Romy studied her hands. Then he finally spoke, steady but low.

'I go to the city. About four times a year…'

She lifted her eyes to his profile. Was he finally going to share something with her?

'…to meet with a woman by the name of Adrienne Lucas.'

A vortex opened up deep in Romy's belly.

'Dr Adrienne Lucas of the medical corps. It's a condition of my leave that I check in regularly with her.'

Romy looked up at him, her stomach settling. 'Check in?'

'She's a shrink, Romy. She treats me.'

'What are you on leave for?'

'They call it medical leave. I call it leave of last

resort. It was that or retire from the corps entirely. The corps wanted me to stay.'

'But you didn't want to?'

Silence.

'What happened?'

Clint made a noise in the back of his throat. His fingers beat a steady rhythm on the steering wheel. 'They called us *the force of choice*. One of Australia's elite squadrons. It meant we were posted deep inside conflicts all over the world. Reconnaissance, retrieval, extractions. We saw things no one should have to look at. Eventually you get used to seeing those things. And to doing them.'

Romy slid her hand over towards him until her little finger barely touched his thigh. She very much needed some part of her to be touching some part of him.

'One day I saw something I couldn't get used to. One of my patrol committed something so...' He shook his head, took a deep breath. 'A kid, no older than Leighton. It was unacceptable. We were supposed to be helping people. There was only the two of us on reconnaissance, the LT and me. I didn't want to dog on a senior, a friend, but I didn't know what else to do.

'I talked to the LT about it. We were pretty tight. He seemed remorseful, said he appreciated me coming direct to him. Grateful enough that I'd handled it discreetly he granted me a weekend leave.' He shook his head in the darkness. 'I spent most of it drunk in the desert, trying to erase what I'd seen from my mind. When I got back to base, I got carpeted by my CO.'

'What happened?'

'LT cited me for bailing during the mission. He said I didn't have what it took in close combat. It became my superior's word against my own. I was forced to justify myself, forced to tell them what happened with the kid, that he was only defending his family with a rusty old AK with no ammo in it.' His voice thickened.

Romy stared at him. 'They didn't believe you.'

'There was a reason we all looked up to the LT. He was the best, a talented strategist.' His laugh turned ugly. 'He struck pre-emptively to undermine everything I said. He painted me as a coward, made sure the whole platoon heard about it.'

'And they believed that? About a man who'd earned a commendation for valour?' He fell to silence. Romy realised. 'You wore it. You didn't challenge him.' As a woman who spent her life feeling judged, she knew exactly how to say that. Factual. Simple. Toneless. He'd find no judgement here.

'I thought I could tough it out, watch the LT, try and prevent anything like it from happening again. But the other troopers in my unit, men who'd trusted me with their lives, suddenly didn't want to know me.' He clenched the steering wheel as if it was a weapon. 'I was dropped to solo recon. And the LT kept on going out.'

He sounded like a man and a wounded animal all

at once. Romy got a real sense of how important that trust relationship was to him. How badly his loyalty had been abused.

'When did you leave?' she asked.

'He finally went too far. Command pulled him out and it all came to the surface. What I saw was just the tip of the iceberg. Even they were shocked, I think. My XO hustled to make good on the damage done, but nothing could undo it for me. I'd grown suspicious of everyone. I had no faith in the men I served with. I had no faith in myself. I started to believe...'

Whatever he'd been about to say, he couldn't finish. He looked stricken. 'I spent the best part of a year drunk whenever I wasn't on mission. It was the only way I could sleep at night.'

'So you went on leave?'

'Command considers it some kind of compensation. Either that or they didn't want a flaming star medallist cut loose and drawing attention. In any case I'm pensioned off on medical leave until my time is up, then they'll discharge me honourably with no fuss. It's all over.'

She picked her way through a minefield of possible responses and, as was her peculiar talent, selected the most painful one. 'But not for you?'

His eyes blazed like emerald coals. 'That unit was my family, Romy. I would have died for any one of them and I nearly did, several times. So to be turned on by the men who I would have taken a bullet for...

To have the corps call my courage into question, my honour…'

Death before dishonour.

Romy shuddered. He'd watched his mother desert his father; then his lieutenant betrayed him, his brothers-in-arms turned on him, his corps abandoned him. The only person he had in the world was Justin. The already strong brotherly bond doubled.

Amazing he could still function, really. That spoke of enormous strength behind those fathomless eyes. She slid her hand onto his where it gripped the steering wheel desperately.

A road train thundered by, its long string of side-lights casting an eerie glow onto his face. He glanced down at her fingers on his and pulled them free. He returned his attention to the dark road and started the car.

She stared at his tortured profile. There was more. Something she was missing. This was about more than just Clint.

'Is he still inside the system? Your lieutenant?'

Clint snorted. 'Deep inside it. Brig-deep. He won't be seeing the outside of a military prison for another decade.'

'Good. He deserves it.'

'Maybe we both do.'

She sucked in a quiet breath. 'You blame yourself for the boy that died.'

The silence stretched for an eternity. 'But for some geography, that could have been Leighton.' His voice was thick and low. 'Just a regular little kid before the conflict started. The only one left to defend his mother and sisters. Terrified.'

The image of Leighton bleeding to death into the desert sands trying to protect her roiled from her brain to her stomach. She cleared her throat. 'You didn't kill him.'

'I didn't save him.'

'You can't be responsible for every child. Every loss.'

Romy's heart ached for the pain she saw etched there. Then he spoke again, as if he couldn't seal off the floodgate now he'd opened it.

'I nearly killed Justin once.' Her shocked silence was question enough. 'In the dam down from your cottage. I was supposed to be watching him. I was showing off for some local girls whose parents were visiting mine. Older girls. Pretty girls.'

Her whispered words were measured. 'He got in trouble in the water?'

'He was struggling in the water. I didn't notice for nearly a minute.'

Romy's hand slid up onto his leg. Entirely inadequate.

Sixty seconds without oxygen...

'One of the girls was a pool attendant in the city in the summer holidays. She resuscitated him after I pulled him out. He was only five.'

Making Clint only thirteen. Still a child himself.

Too young to take on that guilt. Too young not to. 'You mentioned that you owed him.'

'His development was slowed after that. For years it looked like he'd never be able to learn like everyone else.' His bitter smile twisted. 'The man Mum ran off to the States with was Justin's developmental specialist.'

Charming.

'He seems pretty normal now.' Romy suppressed the memory of the nasty glint in Justin's eyes at the dance. No wonder Clint was protective of his brother. He'd probably spent a lifetime being subtly reminded of what had nearly happened. Empathy welled up for the guilt-ridden young man Clint must have been. The damaged man he'd grown into. She cleared her throat. 'If he got a front-of-house role in a major hotel, Justin can't have had much lasting damage.'

He nodded, slow and thoughtful. 'Pure luck. And skill on the part of Richard Long, my stepfather. It could have been very different.'

Romy took the opportunity. She lightened her words. Carefully, carefully… 'He doesn't really talk about it much. His US job.'

Clint slid his glance sideways. 'Leave it, Romy. Stop fishing for mystery you won't find.'

'I'm just curious.' *Because the Joliet Grovesnor had no record of a concierge called Justin Long. Or Justin McLeish.* And that's where Simone said he'd earned his management stripes. 'I'd like to know more about how they run the big US hotels.'

'Then ask him.'

The idea of having a reasonable conversation with Justin Long was laughable. Even before she'd half crippled him with her Vulcan death grip. But if he was lying to Clint, she wanted to know about it. It was her job. 'I might just do that.'

The past fifteen minutes explained so much. Why wouldn't you shut yourself away after an incident like he'd experienced in the military? Who *would* you trust?

She thought about her father and what sorts of things he must have seen in his time in active service, what that might do to a man. How it must take extra strength even to do the day-to-day things, never mind the horrendous things they were tasked with. Had her father done any of that? She thought about how there was no weapon on this earth strong enough to fight the infection which took her mother, and how a control freak like the Colonel must have felt about being powerless. About the baby whose birth caused the deadly, aggressive infection.

She frowned.

Clint had been ripped out of his unit, away from the men he was closest to, and look how it had affected him. The Colonel was recalled unexpectedly from active duty to come home and raise a motherless infant single-handed and assigned forever after to passive training and admin roles. It didn't change one moment of the misery that was her childhood, but it did make her appreciate, a tiny bit, how it must have been for the Colonel twenty-six years ago.

And why he might have viewed her as the enemy her whole life.

CHAPTER NINE

LEAVING Romy alone, injured and patently conflicted, on her front verandah last night had been one of
the hardest things Clint had done since coming to
WildSprings. Every part of him wanted to scoop her
up and carry her inside. Tuck her into bed. Bind her
ankle. Spoil her. Instead, he'd locked her car up and
footed the mile home in the dark, walking off some
of his tension.

It had helped. A little.

The morning coffee was helping more. He sipped
the battery-acid-strength brew.

Romy had a way of bringing out the caveman in
him and then making him feel ridiculous for it. And
he didn't feel like overtures of kindness would be wel-
comed from him. Not after he'd near mauled her back
at the fundraiser. Thanks to her father, she was highly
sensitised to being dominated. She saw it at every turn.
He didn't want her connecting him with those feelings.
Ever.

He didn't want to be responsible for shadows in her
eyes. Or her son's.

A sudden knock at the door had him leaping for the Browning nine-millmetre sidearm he didn't carry any more. The fact someone got all the way to his door without being detected… He was losing his touch. He pulled it open.

'Hi, Clint. Can I come in?'

Justin seemed distracted, and this was the first time in months his brother had visited the tree house. Something was up. Clint stood aside and waved him in.

Justin shuffled nervously in the doorway. 'I need to talk to you. About last night.'

Clint's heart kicked into gear. Had someone seen him and Romy? Probably. Not exactly his most covert operation. He steeled himself for the inevitable attack.

He crossed to the kitchen and held up his mug. 'Coffee?'

Justin winced and shook his head. 'I won't say no to a hair of the dog, though.'

Clint reached into the fridge for a beer, then glanced at the clock on the microwave. It was barely 9:00 a.m. Concern had him frowning but he passed the bottle to his brother. They moved out to the balcony—still haunted by the ghost of Romy's recent visit. Being alone out here was no longer the refuge it once was.

'Spit it out,' Clint growled.

Justin lifted red-flecked eyes. 'It's about Romy…'

Thump, thump, thump… The pulsing was hard and fast in his chest. 'What about her?'

'I...' Justin swore and slumped down onto the nearest seat, taking a big swig of beer. 'I hit on her.'

The thumping stopped. For near on five painful seconds. When it returned, Clint forced it to be slow and steady. The same heartbeat he regulated when his finger was hovering over the hair-trigger. But it was a battle he almost lost.

Justin met his eyes but couldn't hold them. He pushed up off his seat and crossed to the balustrade. 'I was drunk, mate. I wasn't thinking.'

Silence was Clint's only option. If he spoke he'd say too much. Justin babbled on, filling the tense vacuum.

'She looked hot, Clint. She was playing up to every man there. Even you.'

Breathe...breathe... 'What did you do, exactly?'

Justin swung around to look at him. Suspicion and disbelief in his eyes. 'She really hasn't told you?'

'She didn't. No. Did you expect her to?'

He swore again. 'I'm sure she's just picking her moment.'

Clint kept his voice even. 'I'm sure she's not. She likes to fight her own battles.'

'Tell me about it. She nearly broke my shoulder when I touched her.'

Clint would normally have grinned at his brother's petulant complaint, and the image of Romy strongarming all six feet of him. He pressed his lips together. 'Why are you telling me?'

Justin sighed, waved his hands dramatically. 'Harassment laws. She's our employee.'

Something I should have thought about last night. And the night they'd stood out here on the balcony.

'Then shouldn't you be apologising to her right now instead of confessing your sins to me?' Clint suggested, and then his chest tightened almost painfully. *No.* He didn't want Justin anywhere near Romy's place.

His brother rolled his eyes and Clint was reminded of a much younger version, the excitable young Justin he didn't see a lot of any more. He frowned. Time had changed them both.

'She's a woman.' Justin shrugged. 'She'll find some insidious way to get her revenge. Warn every chick in the district off me. Put salt in the sugar shaker. Start spreading rumours.'

Clint stared. Shook his head. 'You really are still sixteen, aren't you?'

'Mate, I give her two days before she starts turning everyone against me.'

Clint reached over and confiscated the beer bottle from his hands. 'You're paranoid. Take the day to dry out. If you hit on her last night, then you're going to have to wear the consequences like a man, even if that means drinking your coffee salted.'

Justin stood to go. At the door, Clint stopped him. 'Oh, and, mate…?'

Justin turned back, a satisfied smile on his face. It faded as he took in his big brother's expression.

'Touch her again and I'll do a hell of a lot worse than break your shoulder.'

Romy had nearly forgotten what Leighton's scowl looked like. But this one was a pearler and it was all for her.

He'd been a changed boy since coming to WildSprings. Happier, more open…huggier. Not today. Today he was a tiny black thundercloud glaring at her whenever she made eye contact, his heart well and truly plastered on his sleeve. His breakfast entirely untouched.

'Leighton, if you're done eating, scrape your eggs into the compost and put the plate on the sink, please.' Given everything that had gone on these past few days, her own mood wasn't the best.

He slid off his seat like a blob of the green slime he'd used to love to play with, mumbling, 'Yes, ma'am.' One hundred and ten percent surly.

Her hands stilled on what she was doing. She took a small breath. 'That's "Yes, Mum" to you, mister.'

His glare compounded. 'Soldiers say *ma'am*. It's polite.'

She straightened uncomfortably. 'Last time I checked you weren't a soldier.'

'I'm gonna be.' His defiant glare was magnified by the lenses in his small round glasses.

Don't bite. Don't bite…

She kept her voice painfully level. 'What happened to being a scientist?'

A hint of uncertainty flashed across those freckled cheeks. 'Science is for geeks.'

Romy turned and looked him square in the eye. She'd worked long and hard to instil a sense of pride in her son for his special talents with wildlife, astronomy, computers—all things geeky.

We don't get to choose our gifts. Leighton running his abilities down worried her. Was he getting this from school?

'Is that right?' she said, carefully neutral.

'I'm going to be an artilleryman.'

Her heart began to pound, high in her throat. 'You want to shoot guns for a living?'

'Every soldier needs to be good with a gun. It's for survival. Clint is a soldier.'

'Who told you that?'

'And my granddad was a soldier.'

She gripped the benchtop behind her, breathless. Who told him *that*?

'And I'm gonna be a soldier, too,' Leighton finished on a very defiant stare.

A hint of acid rose in Romy's throat and she sagged against the edge of the bench. *Damn you, Clint McLeish. He's only a child....*

She pulled herself back up. 'Not for another ten years you're not. Until then, the only orders you'll be taking are from me, young man.'

'Nuh-uh!' Those small grey eyes burned with defiance.

Romy had a sudden memory of challenging the

Colonel, her pint-size body stiff, arguing about things she couldn't possibly have understood. Her lips thinned. 'What has gotten into you, Leighton Carvell? You never speak this rudely to anyone!'

His eyes watered dangerously behind his glasses and his little round face boiled red with rage and then paled just as dramatically. He blinked back the tears. 'Why doesn't Clint come around any more?'

That took her by surprise. She stared at him, her anger dissolving instantly. 'It's only been three days, L. He's probably...busy.'

'He was supposed to take me on a bushwalk. He promised. Now he won't come because of you.'

Oh, God, she'd let Clint get too close... *Stupid, stupid!* 'Who says he won't?'

Leighton's baleful stare grew cautious. 'You went on a date and now he won't come.'

It sounded so ludicrous Romy wanted to laugh. But it was embarrassingly close to the truth. 'No. We did not go on a date. We went to a work thing together. And I don't know why he hasn't been around since then. It's a coincidence.'

Great, now you're lying to your own son.

Then again, it took two to tango—the wide, circling part of tango in their case. She knew why she was keeping her distance. How could she be with him and not have her heart very obviously on her sleeve? But if Clint had wanted to see her...he was right next door.

She sighed. 'I'll see if I can get in touch, ask him about the walk. Maybe he's planning it already?'

A battle twisted Leighton's face. He wanted to be ecstatic, but he also tried to be cool about it, and he was still so mad. The result was a pinched half-grimace that helped Romy remember exactly how it felt to be a young child growing up conflicted. Confused. Disappointed.

She'd never wanted him to feel that. She knelt in front of him and held her arms out. 'Okay, L?'

He didn't rush into them, but he didn't walk off either. He let himself lean forwards as her arms closed around him and then he rested his cheek on her shoulder and mumbled something that might have been 'Thanks, Mum.'

'Grab your school bag. I'll drop you down to the bus.' She patted his bottom and gave him a gentle push in the direction of the stairs. He needed space and some friends around him right now, much more than he needed his trembling wreck of a mother. He'd have a heap of confusing emotions to work through.

And so did she.

Part of her wanted to slap Clint for talking about the military in front of Leighton. The very last thing in this world she wanted was for her precious angel to start getting interested in the same kind of lifestyle that had made her life a living hell. Another part of her knew her son was his own person, not hers to dictate to. Hadn't that been what she fought against her whole, short childhood? He wouldn't be the first boy to develop a fixation for toy guns and soldiers.

She frowned, realising that he *had* demonstrated this

interest before. Back in third grade, when he'd asked about joining the junior orienteering team, she'd persuaded him to join the astronomy club instead. Simply because orienteering involved mapping and compass work and treks through the bush.

Like an army cadet programme.

She snatched her keys off the bench and limped through the screen door on her nearly healed ankle just as Leighton came bounding down the stairs. She glanced at his now-rosy cheeks and chewed her lip. How long had she been unconsciously guiding him away from any interest remotely like military activity? He'd done it, subjugated his preference for hers and joined astronomy. Because she wanted him to. What kind of a mother did that make her?

The Colonel's daughter?

Romy kept her arm high, waving Leighton off, until the bus trundled right off into the distance. She'd make it up to him tonight, try and put their relationship back together as it used to be. She'd promised him a mother-son movie night with special treats and a kid's action-adventure flick. He loved those.

She frowned again.

He loved those. Lord, how many clues was she missing?

She ducked her head and walked the hundred metres from the bus stop to WildSprings's admin centre, to her broom closet of an office. She had some invoices to sign off and a vehicle registration to run past her police contact at Central.

She finished detailing the vehicle type and plate number and addressed the email. Then she turned her attention, reluctantly, to a pile of invoices sitting in her in-tray from Friday. Testament to how distracted she'd been that day about her big night out with Clint.

Not *with* Clint... Even now her subconscious was pulling them together. After everything that had happened at the fundraiser and everything they'd said in the car afterwards. She had never shared the details of Leighton's conception with anyone. Including her father. That was a private shame just for her. Even at seventeen she'd been responsible enough to accept her actions and live with them. Lying in the bed she'd made—literally. It was blind luck she'd ended up with a child and not something more life threatening for her poor judgement.

It had taken the Colonel several months to catch on to her pregnancy. She'd hidden the early symptoms well during her final weeks of school and, having been lean all her life, she hadn't shown until her fourth month. But once he'd realised...

But his anger then hadn't been a patch on his rage when her military hospital robe had exposed her tattoo. Her *obscenity*. He seemed more appalled by that than by the life growing inside her. In the end, it was the cost—and not the certain pain—which made the Colonel back down from the threat of having it burned right off her skin.

Dr Pax won no favours from her father after he admired the quality of the tattoo artwork but he won a shy smile from a tear-streaked Romy. And she'd trusted him enough to return privately for the essential prenatal care she otherwise wouldn't have sought out. She'd really liked Dr Pax.

Romy's head snapped up.

She'd really *liked* Dr Pax. He was kind and gentle but disciplined, too. And he was a military doctor. Which meant he'd been through the system. Yet come out the other side a decent human being. Someone she'd genuinely respected. Someone who's authority she had no difficulty accepting. The breath puffed out of her and Romy sat back in her chair and stared at the roof, poleaxed.

Dr Pax...Clint. That made two-thirds of the military men she'd ever met compassionate, kind and gentle. Men she didn't have trouble liking. A clear majority.

Her father was the exception, not the rule!

She thought back to the way Clint had shielded her body with his in the doorway, how he'd fussed around her injured ankle, how he'd kissed away her tears in his tree house. Yes, he was capable of great passion, too—she remembered the angry blaze of his eyes all too clearly—but essentially his military side and his human side existed in reasonable harmony. Despite the great trials he'd been through.

And look how he was with Leighton. Firm, but fair. Patient. Gentle.

He may well kill for those he loved, but he was at

least capable of deeper emotion. For the first time, she wondered if perhaps her father would have been a difficult man to love even without his military background.

'Looking for breaches of security in the ceiling panels, Romy?'

Her body stiffened with sudden tension. It was too soon. She pushed herself to her feet. 'Clint...'

'How are you?' His words weren't exactly cold but they were a long way from warm.

'I'm fine, thank you.' Oh, so painfully polite. 'Is there something you need?'

He stepped into her tiny office and closed the door. Her blood pressure rose instantly. 'I need to ask you about something.'

'Actually, I need to ask you something, too.' *Stay away from my son.*

He leaned on the doorframe, tipped his head towards her.

She took a deep breath. 'Why have you been talking to Leighton about being in the military?'

He frowned. 'I haven't.'

Who else would have? 'He knows you were a soldier. Now he wants to be one.'

He studied her carefully. 'Then it's not from me. And you know I can't agree that's a terrible thing.'

'Despite everything you've been through?'

He nodded. 'Even so. But that doesn't mean I talk to him about it. I can barely talk to my shrink about it—do you imagine I offload onto an eight-year-old boy?'

She frowned. 'You told me about it.'

Caution slammed down over his eyes. 'Inappropriate impulse.'

Oh. Awkward silence fell between them. She rushed to cover the pang his words caused. 'I don't want him idolising you. What you were.'

'Yes, because that would be a crime. Seeing as I'm pond scum in your eyes.'

Her heart squeezed. 'You know that's not true.'

His irises bled to the green of a storm-tossed dam. 'I appreciate your upbringing was a very difficult one and I can understand how that might have left you with a skewed view of the military,' he said. 'But I happen to be enormously proud of the work I did in the Defence Force, the lives I saved and the difference I made to my country…'

'Clint—'

'I can't suppress that for you, Romy. It's a part of who I am and I'm through apologising for it. I am a member of the Australian Armed Forces, proud to have served my country, proud of my actions in conflict and proud to still belong to Strike Force Taipan in whatever capacity I can be. Deal with it.'

And there it was. Out in the open. Only he looked as surprised to have said it as she was to hear it.

The ball of tension in her chest tumbled and rolled and trebled in size, pushing on her heart and swelling with pride. Pride for Clint. It was far more important that he accept that part of him than she did. She nodded.

'Okay.'

'Okay...? That's it?'

It physically hurt to speak. 'You shouldn't apologise for doing something you believe in wholeheartedly. Your core values. I won't ask you to.'

'You ask me in a hundred little ways, Romy. I feel it every time I'm with you.'

Shame washed through her. That's how she used to feel with her father. She heaved in an unsteady breath and tried to move away from her desk but there was not far to go when he was taking up so much of the room. 'What did you need to see me for?' she finally got out, needing to move to safer territory.

He glared at her, dark and intense. Veiled. Not surprising given their parting on Friday night. 'Do you trust me, Romy?'

With my life. 'Wh...why?'

'You didn't tell me about my brother.'

Romy frowned and glanced at her computer screen. How did he know? 'Uh, there wasn't much to tell before today.' *Before she got this morning's email from her contact in Chicago.*

'Did you think I wouldn't believe you?'

'I...' She shook her head to clear the confusion. She pulled her focus off his overwhelming presence in her miniature office. 'He's your brother... I didn't want to—'

'Tell me now. I want to hear it.'

Lord... She'd wanted time to prepare for this...to even work out what it could mean. It wasn't something you just announced. But he was asking. Waiting.

She reached into a low drawer and pulled a file out, then passed the sheet on the top to Clint. 'Justin never worked at the Joliet Grosvenor.'

His eyes froze over on the paper and she hurried on. 'There's no record of him even being registered in the Hospitality Association in Chicago. He would have to have been, to work front desk in a major hotel.'

'What is this?' His voice was as brittle as the orchards in a frost.

Confusion muddled her mind. 'Justin never worked—'

'I heard what you said.' He raised pained eyes to hers and shook the paper. The blaze in his eyes could have combusted it in his hand. 'You investigated my brother?'

Her breath stopped. The room shrank around her and an enormous hole opened up inside her. 'What were *you* talking about?'

'Justin behaving...inappropriately at the fund-raiser.'

Octopus hands were just a blip on her radar compared to what came after with Clint. She'd all but forgotten Justin's drunken pawing.

A deep scowl dropped over the angles of his face. 'Why the hell are you investigating my brother?'

Romy could have apologised. Begged his forgiveness. But when her antennae were vibrating so wildly she knew better than to back down. There was too much at stake. Clint's heart. She took a bolstering breath around the tightness in her chest. 'Why would he lie to you?'

'Am I part of your investigation now?'

She took the hit. Prepared herself for more. To protect him. 'Why would he lie, Clint?'

'Who says he is lying?'

'The Government of the United States. My contact's in a Federal department in Chicago.'

He prowled around her broom-closet office, then doubled back on her. 'Overkill, don't you think?'

Actually, yes, it was. Majorly. 'I contacted Carly as a friend, not a Federal officer.'

'Why?'

'Because there's something not right about Justin—'

His colour blanched slightly. 'I've told you why that is. The near-drowning…'

Desperation started to pick at her fringes. Had she overreacted? Could she be wrong about Justin? She forced the doubt away. 'Clint. Forget that he's your brother, just for a moment. *Why* would he lie about his background?'

Clint finally lifted tortured eyes to her. 'You've certainly wasted no time in getting your revenge.'

'Revenge for what?'

'For him trying it on with you.'

Hurt slammed through her. 'You think that's what this is?'

'You tell me. First you tell me he hit on you, then you tell me he's a liar.'

Her pulse started to hammer at the accusation in his voice. 'I never told you he hit on me. *You* brought it up.'

Clint glared. 'Actually, *he* did. He owned up to it immediately. Expressed his regret. Like a man.'

Her chest heaved with barely restrained anger. 'How good of him. Have you not given any thought to *why* he might do that? What he had to gain?'

Clint shook his head. It matched the tremble in his hands. 'I feel sure you're about to tell me.'

Grief thickened her voice. Something beautiful was dying. Romy could feel it slipping through her helpless fingers. 'Do I really have to tell you about pre-emptive strikes? Justin knew you'd take him to pieces when you found out he'd touched me and so he was getting in first. Shoring up support.' Shields she hadn't had to employ in some time started to creak back into position. The familiar thick, lead-lined walls that protected her for so much of her childhood. 'It was pure strategy, Clint. He's clever.'

He launched away from her, as far as he could get in the tiny room. 'Make up your mind, Romy. One minute he's damaged, the next he's Einstein.' He swung back to burn down on her. 'There's something I don't understand. If you're so determined to come between us why didn't you tell me about him hitting on you yourself?'

Because his brother's touch blew everything else

from my mind, eclipsed everything that came before it. 'Maybe because his weren't the only hands I had on me that night!'

But one look at his bleached face and she knew how it sounded. Her stomach contracted.

'Clint…'

He cut her off physically, pushing past her to leave the office. He threw the offending report onto her desk. 'Stay the hell away from my family.'

CHAPTER TEN

'CLINT'S here! Clint's here!'

A human cannonball came thundering down the stairs two at a time. Romy froze where she was standing, in the midst of lighting her living room candles. She lit them every evening, an array of subtle, scented lights to ease away the worries of the day and fill her environment with beauty. Tonight she'd lit double.

It still wasn't enough.

Leighton flung the door open before Clint even had a chance to knock. He hurled himself at the jean-clad legs, more like the little boy he had been last week. Her heart squeezed to see someone else making her son so happy. Wasn't that her job?

'Hey, champ, how are you doing?'

She hated the light, relaxed tone he employed with her son. It was so different to the way he spoke to her.

Leighton bounced at his feet. 'Have you come to take me on our bushwalk? Mum said she was going to ask you.'

Clint's cold green stare met hers. Her lashes swept

down. Lord, she'd completely forgotten her promise to her son.

'Sure did, champ,' he covered smoothly, 'and your mum, too.' There was the barest pause before he added, 'If she wants to come.'

Romy wasn't certain which of them looked less enthusiastic about that. Possibly even herself. Spending time with Clint was the very last thing she wanted to do.

'Right now?' she hedged.

'Unless you have something more important to be doing.' *Like lighting candles,* his raised eyebrow seemed to say.

'Yay!' Leighton leapt back into the house and scampered up the stairs.

Romy raced through her options. She could beg off, blame her ankle, but that meant leaving her son with Clint unsupervised, and he was just as likely to teach him how to shoot something if she wasn't there to stop it. Prohibiting Leighton from going would destroy what little repair work she'd managed to do to their relationship. Or she *could* go. Endure two hours in Clint's company like an adult and try not to say something that might get her fired.

Leighton reappeared in the kitchen carrying his hiking boots. She smiled at him brightly. 'What about our movie night?' It was worth a shot.

He looked at her, crestfallen. 'Can't we watch the movie tomorrow night, Mum?'

That sweet face broke her. She knew only too well

how it felt to try and please everyone all of the time. The pressure that put on little shoulders.

She sighed. 'Okay, let me blow these candles out…'

Leighton let out another cheer and burst out the door, leaving Clint standing alone in the kitchen.

'Let me help you with that,' he said tightly.

'No, thanks. I've got it.' Her puffs of air were quick and efficient and extinguished each candle as if, with every one, she snuffed out one of her complex feelings for the man hovering in her doorway.

'Romy…'

She spun around and faced him. What was he going to say? *Sorry I ripped your heart out and threw it against the wall. My mistake. Can you ever forgive me?*

Her stare felt as dead as her heart. 'I assumed when you told me to stay away from your family, it was a given you'd stay away from mine.'

He sighed and dropped his gaze to the floor. 'He's my *brother*, Romy. You investigated him based on nothing but a gut feeling.'

'Accurate gut feeling.'

'It's not an insignificant thing.'

She didn't want to see the sense in that. She didn't want to let him off the hook. Hurting was too good. Like vindication for every suspicion she'd ever had about Clint McLeish and his values. The aching tooth you can't leave alone.

'You employed me to protect WildSprings and you

are WildSprings, Clint. I'm trying to protect you,' she whispered, conscious of little ears nearby.

'I don't need protection, Romy. Not from my brother.'

'You don't know that.'

'I do.' His lips pressed together and he shook his head. 'For someone who dislikes being judged so much,' he went on, 'you do a pretty good job of judging others.'

Fury boiled between them like a natural spring. But just as she opened her mouth to let him have it, Leighton bounced back into the house. He glanced from one to the other and some of the glow dimmed in his cheeks. He looked anxious. 'Are we still going?'

Romy immediately turned her focus onto her son with a bright smile. 'Yep, good to go. Which way are we headed?'

Leighton looked to Clint for an answer.

'I thought I'd take you around to the next gully. Out towards the roosting site,' he said. 'Would you like to see where the cockatoos sleep, champ?'

'Yeah!' Leighton burst out the door again.

Clint turned back to say something further but Romy locked her gaze somewhere over his shoulder and studied the kitchen wall. Her voice was frigid.

'Let's go.'

The route to the roosting site, as the crow flew, was shorter than the track he and Romy had taken by car. Nevertheless, the bushwalk nearly killed Clint.

He was still mission fit—being on four-hour call perpetually was a hard habit to break—so it wasn't the cross-country trek down the heart of the gully that took so much out of him. It was the silence that grew exhausting, almost unendurable. It was nothing like the crucial silence he maintained while on mission, nor the comfortable one he enjoyed with Leighton— two mates, twenty years between them, hanging out. It was the draining, stressful silence of two people who'd wounded each other too badly to undo. Two dogs starved into fighting who don't have the heart or the energy to finish each other.

His nerves were still frayed from the days of non-contact. Romy avoiding him was all too similar to the men in his unit steering clear of him after he'd dogged on their lieutenant. In his head he knew it was probably for the best, that there was no future for them, regardless of the killer chemistry they shared. But in his heart…

Walking between them, Leighton kept up a relentless stream of innocent questions about the bush, wildlife, the park. Clint did his best to answer while his mother maintained a stony silence. But as the evening sun dropped closer to the tree line and the mosquitoes moved in, Clint realised the questions were becoming more strategic. Less about bush-craft and more about military field-craft.

How do you move so quietly through the trees?
How can you tell which way a noise is coming from?

What colours are best to wear for camouflage in the forest?

How about the desert?

And every question he asked caused Romy's spine to ratchet that little bit tighter until her determined strides through the trees looked plain uncomfortable.

He knew what Leighton was doing. He remembered his parents' flawed relationship, trying to work out what was up with the two most important people in *his* life. He'd poked and poked at the open wound of their marriage until it bled so he could comprehend it better.

Leighton was just doing some good old-fashioned reconnaissance, eight-year-old style—trying to provoke a reaction so he could study the response. He'd make a great scientist. And a better soldier.

Over his mother's dead body.

He glanced at Romy's steely expression.

And very possibly his.

CHAPTER ELEVEN

ROMY shifted uncomfortably for the sixteenth time. Her kitchen chairs were certainly not built for long-term occupation. She flexed her aching back and did a couple of quick stretches to give her a moment away from her laptop. The longer she stared, the less meaningful the images became. A jumbled montage of maps and highlighted points. She pushed all the paper maps away, too.

'Whatcha doing?' Leighton crash-landed in the chair next to hers, peering over her shoulder.

'Trying to figure out who hit that kangaroo.' She'd told her son all about it, hoping to win his interest back over to wildlife appreciation. It hadn't worked. He was still fixated with Clint and all things military.

'Why? Isn't it too late now?'

'Maybe I can stop them doing it again. A chance to educate someone.' Much as she'd like to wring their irresponsible neck. She rubbed her knotted shoulder.

Leighton's sharp eyes missed nothing. 'Is it hard work?'

She blew out a breath and then smiled at the worry

in his eyes. The protectiveness. Every day, more and more a young man. 'I just feel like I'm missing something. Like it's…right there…' She tapped her forehead, then shook it.

'Do you want to read it out loud?'

She always made Leighton read words he didn't understand aloud, to help with comprehension. After the tension they'd had between them this week she was just happy to be having a normal conversation with him. *Grab it while you can—even if it means putting work off for a while.*

She smiled. 'Can you spare a few minutes?'

He scooted in closer. 'Sure. It's better than math home-work.'

If she was half the smooth operator she believed she was, she'd find a way to sneak in a mathematical principle or two while she was at it. She stretched out one of the maps. 'Okay. So this is WildSprings.' She pointed to the west of the map. 'This is the admissions area where I work. This is our house…and Clint's… and over here's where I'm spending a *lot* of time.'

'Is that the fence you keep fixing?'

'That's the one.' She glanced at his eager, interested face. 'So, knowing that, can you show me where Frog Swamp is?'

He pointed immediately to a point just south of their house. She smiled. 'And what's the fastest way from our place to Clint's?'

Bright eyes turned up to her. 'On foot or by car?'

She smiled. *Oh, clever boy.* 'Foot.'

He stared hard at the map. 'Is this the gully? The one we walked up to get to the roosting site? Which means Clint's house is…there?'

Romy glanced at the map, somewhat surprised he'd found it. 'Well done. Yes, it is.' Now on with her only semihypothetical problem. 'And *this* is where we found the kangaroo.' She pointed to a spot about halfway between the roosting site and the part of the fence that was fast becoming her second home.

His little brows folded in and he shoved his glasses more firmly onto his nose. Her heart squeezed. It had been a long time since she'd seen him so…engaged. She frowned.

'Go on, Mum…'

She cleared her throat. 'We were heading east from the roosting site when we found the roo. So, assuming the yahoos got in through the breach in the fence over here—' she pointed to the east of WildSprings '—we should have passed them after they hit the roo. But we didn't see them, so where did they go?'

Leighton stared at the map, his little eyes darting all over it. 'Could they have hidden anywhere?'

Adorable. He was taking this so seriously. Romy did the same, focusing on keeping the smile from her face. 'Not likely. Clint and I would both have noticed tracks running off the road.'

She sat back and watched her son computing. His little fingers mimicked hers, tracing back and forth over the features of the map, nearly hunched over in concentration trying to solve the puzzle. After an eternity he sat straight and looked at her.

'Do they have to be coming in the hole in the fence?'

Ah, good boy. Question the variables. The kid was a natural scientist. 'I guess they could have come through WildSprings's main entrance—'

'No. I mean…can't they be going *out* through the fence?'

Cold ice washed through Romy as she stared at her brilliant, *brilliant* son. It was so sensationally obvious.

It wasn't a shortcut in; it was a shortcut out.

Her eyes narrowed. Breaking *in* was just petty vandalism. Idiots out hooning or showing off for their girlfriends. Someone secretly *leaving* the exclusive property felt a whole lot more sinister. Romy swivelled the map back towards her and let her eyes run from the breach in the fence, past the roo strike site to the roost site. Then back again.

Her eyes widened and she kissed the ginger head beside her. 'Leighton, you're a genius! Time for bed.'

His wail was almost comic. 'But I helped you!'

'Yes, you did. But until you invent a tool to bend time, then it's still eight o'clock. Bedtime. Scoot.'

The bright, eager shine in his eyes dulled to a rebellious storm cloud. A storm cloud rapidly preparing to break open. Romy felt the familiar tightening in her chest, the kick in her pulse. It wasn't the same feeling she used to experience with her father but it was a close cousin. Not fear that she couldn't control Leighton, but fear that she might. And not in a good way.

She took a breath and tried to channel Clint. Firm but fair. 'Twenty minutes of reading once you're in your pyjamas. Then lights out.'

The storm didn't clear, but it didn't break. He skulked to the base of the stairs.

'And, Leighton?' she went on as his foot hit the first tread. 'Thank you. You've really, really helped.'

He didn't let her off the hook, but his back grew a tad straighter and his footfalls were lighter as he sprinted up the stairs.

Some of the tension drained from her body. But not all of it.

She spun the laptop towards herself and fired up her wireless email. The boys from Customs wouldn't get it until the morning but alerting them to a possible issue required due diligence. Better that they have WildSprings on their radar than not.

She was two-thirds of the way through detailing the recent incident when her laptop pinged to let her know it had finished loading her incoming mail. She glanced down to see who the new mail was from. There were two. Darren from Police, and Carly from Chicago.

She flicked open Darren's first and stared, disbelieving, at the screen. She took a quick trip from relief to disappointment and then finally confusion.

The 4WD that hit the roo was registered to Clint's brother. Not some intruder up to no good in the park.

Justin. But why hadn't he spoken up? They had a system for reporting wildlife injuries in WildSprings. It wasn't as if it was a criminal offence.

Romy shook her head. She'd be seeing terrorists in the shadows next. Just as well she hadn't sent off her email full of conspiracy theories to Customs. That could have been embarrassing.

She deleted the email she'd spent half an hour composing and then opened Carly's email and started to read.

Her stomach dropped clean away.

'Romy? What's going on? Your message sounded urgent.'

She trembled from more than the cool night air. Adrenaline. Anxiety. How on earth was she going to start this conversation? Knowing what it would do to him.

Thanks for coming, Clint. Oh, by the way, your brother is officially a criminal. Coffee?

He frowned and took her hands. 'You're shaking. Here, sit down.'

She pulled them free of his warmth. Letting it soak in was not going to make this any easier. Look how he reacted last time, not prepared for one second to hear a word against his brother. She crossed her arms across her body and stepped past him, towards the door. 'Can we talk outside, Clint? Leighton's asleep.'

He frowned. 'Sure. Are we planning on getting noisy?'

That was almost a certainty.

'If this is about the other day—'

'It's not,' she whispered, low and shaky. 'At least, not directly. Please, come outside.'

On his parents' little back porch she paced up and down, ordering her thoughts. He watched her closely but didn't speak. Scenarios played out in high-speed in her mind. Different ways this could go. All of them ended in Clint getting hurt.

She finally blurted the easiest part of the story, just for somewhere to start. 'Justin killed that kangaroo.'

His whole body tensed. His lips thinned. 'Romy…'

'Hear me out.' Both her hands shot up and she stepped towards him. 'I found the vehicle that night at the fundraiser when I twisted my ankle. It was Justin's. I just got confirmation from Licensing an hour ago.'

Clint's jaw clamped as he turned away in the half shadows of the porch light. 'You're still on his case?'

'I never was on his case, Clint.' Her heart thundered. She straightened her back as though it would make the slightest difference against six-four of angry man. This was all so horribly familiar. But she had to keep going. 'But I am now.'

'Romy, he regrets it. He told me—'

'Will you listen! This has nothing to do with being felt up by your brother. I didn't even know it *was* your brother I was looking for when I had the plate number analysed. I was just doing my job.'

Clint looked sideways at her, his eyes narrowed.

The man that had the power to make her feel so good could also make her feel bad with one bitter look. She took a steadying breath. It didn't help. 'He hit the kangaroo and then didn't report it.'

A curse tumbled off his lips. 'So sue him, Romy. If he hit the roo, then I'll be giving him a long lecture about responsibility. It's unfortunate but hardly a federal offence.'

If. Even now he had so little faith in her. She steeled herself to continue. To hurt him the way she knew she had to. 'Clint, there's more…'

'Oh, I'll bet there is. You're nothing if not zealous in your pursuit of justice.'

The acid tone served its purpose. She felt the burning judgement as it spattered her. Her throat tightened and she clamped her lips, losing courage.

'No, don't stop now, Romy. Spit it all out. What else has my evil, damaged little brother done to offend?'

The sarcasm sliced her like tumbling scalpels. She wanted to hurl it at him now—the truth about Justin—but she knew she'd only get moments once she started. And hurting Clint was hurting her, doubly. Her chest collapsed in. This could only go one way. She was ripping out both their hearts.

'I'm…I'm worried about the cockatoos. The breach in the fence…' Tremors gave her a weak kind of vibrato. 'I think Justin's connected. The customs memo—'

'Stop!'

He rounded on her then, his eyes a roaring furnace. The blazing fury in his expression burned her.

He advanced and she stumbled over her own feet back into the corner, dipping her head instinctively. It was an ingrained survival technique, but she disgusted herself with her cowardice.

Clint froze. For long, cold, silent seconds. Then he stumbled away from her, her name a curse on his lips.

She fought the sting of tears. Not again. *Not this time.* She lifted her chin and met his wide, horrified gaze with critically dry eyes. Her blood thundered in her ears, her pulse throbbing in her temple, her throat, her mouth. The devastation on his face was nearly her undoing. But he had to know… And he was listening at last.

Her chest throbbed. 'He was expelled from the US on drug charges, Clint. Serious ones. He has a criminal record.'

She watched the emotions play over his features, features she'd come to care for so deeply. The horror, the sorrow, the acceptance. Then he dropped his eyes.

'I know.'

She almost missed his soft confession as an owl screeched in the darkness nearby. She sucked in a lungful of icy, aching air. Stared at him for endless moments until finally able to speak, raw and strained. 'Then why have I torn my heart out to work out how to tell you?'

He sank down on the swing chair. 'He had to come home. It was part of his conditions. That he live with me. Here.'

Romy sagged. *Far from trouble. Under the watchful eye of his highly awarded, ex-military brother.*

Clint went on. 'He wanted a chance to prove himself. To make a fresh start.'

She dropped her head. 'I can understand that.'

'I think we all can.'

More silence. 'You think I'm taking that chance away from him.'

'Aren't you?'

Romy's heart lurched painfully. You'd think she'd have developed some immunity to condemnation after her childhood. 'I'm not doing this to catch Justin out. I'm doing it to protect you.'

He lifted unreadable eyes to hers. 'Why?'

'Because he's going to betray you.' She stared at him steadily. 'And because you love him.'

And because I love you.

Romy's whole body reeled as the words clattered unspoken through her brain. She grabbed at the balustrade and clung to it, trying desperately to look as though she was doing nothing more than collecting her thoughts when in reality she was struggling to breathe. She forced her lungs to inflate. Once. Twice.

Oh, God, no...

'Would you do something for me, Romy?' His flat, lifeless voice brought her head back around. 'If I asked you to...would you drop your investigation? Would you trust me to deal with this my own way?'

Her blood thundered past her ears in torrents and her stomach squeezed into a ball. Everything she'd ever believed in hung suspended in front of her, right next to everything she'd ever wanted. And she couldn't have both. One would make her a traitor to the principles she held most dear. The other would effectively betray Clint.

She looked at the agony in his eyes and her heart answered for her, though it stretched to snapping point. Her conscience lowered its eyes. 'If it was in my power. Yes, I would.' There was no doubt that he'd put his brother's misdeeds to rights. Stop Justin before he did anything to harm anyone more than he already had. But that meant...

'But I can't stay if that happens.' The fracture in her voice echoed the one in her heart and salty tears seeped into her throat through the microscopic fissures. 'I have to think about Leighton. He's all I've got.' He could take whatever risks he wanted to with his business but she was not risking her son.

Clint's eyes fluttered shut. He nodded, his voice thick. 'You should go. Take him far away from here. From me.'

She just nodded. Unable to speak a word for the rigidness in her throat. Knowing what was coming. And what she had to tell him.

Don't ask...don't ask...

He lifted tortured eyes and an invisible sword suspended perilously, aimed at her chest. 'I know what this will mean to you so I wouldn't ask lightly. He's my little brother, Romy. My Leighton.' He took her icy hands in his. 'So I am asking. Will you trust me to deal with this in my own way? Will you let it go?'

For me.

If she said yes she would have to take Leighton away from WildSprings. And if she said no Clint would never forgive her. Her breath shuddered. The Colonel's cruel laughter filled her brain, tight and hysterical.

Either way she was going to lose Clint.

Nausea washed through her in thick waves. As it happened, it was entirely irrelevant. She clenched the timber balustrade behind her for courage. Then she took a breath and fell forwards onto the invisible sword.

'I've already emailed Customs.'

Clint closed his eyes. Dropped his head as though he couldn't tolerate its weight a second longer. As though he'd expected her betrayal. 'Of course you have.'

Panic started to flare deep in her chest. Her voice cracked. 'I had to do what was right—'

'I know.'

His quiet words ended it all. Awful, irreparable stillness fell between them. What else could she say? What else could she expect? They were brothers. And betraying the one that meant nothing to her had betrayed the one that meant everything.

Her voice, when she finally spoke, was deadened with pain she hoped he couldn't hear. 'What do you want me to do?' she whispered.

The night crickets swelled in volume. His dead eyes lifted to lock on hers…and her heart broke.

'You should still go.'

Romy's chest felt as hollow and ancient as the caverns Clint liked to explore. As though everything in it had been suspended in time, waiting for the right man to shine his light and reveal its wonders. As short as it had lasted, it had felt spectacular.

Stupid of her not to have considered what would happen when he climbed on through and out of the cavern.

She swallowed the ache, let it scab over into numbness. 'You still want me to leave?'

He shook his head from side to side slowly, sadly. 'Yes.'

Her voice thickened with unrealised tears. 'Because I exposed your brother?'

'Because you had to.' He lifted gleaming green pools and met her pain head-on. 'I don't want to put you in that position, Romy. Having to choose between me or your values. I've been in that position and I knew what it does to you, long-term.'

Her stomach clenched.

'I can't guarantee we won't be in this position again. My life's pivotal moments are framed by bad decisions.' He spoke more to the night than to her. 'Justin's near-drowning. Not stopping the LT from killing that kid. Dogging on him to Command. Letting my dad leave, alone…'

'You have a flaming star on your wall, Clint.'

He turned hard eyes on her. 'Do you have any idea what I got that for?'

Romy took in the ugly way he held his body. Like it no longer fit him.

'I was shot three times just as my unit was bugging out of a village hot zone. I tied myself to the front of the Humvee and I just kept firing as we reversed at high speed back into the desert.'

'What's unworthy about that? It sounds extraordinary.'

'I strapped myself in with the rifle straps of my dead buddies so I wouldn't be left behind if I passed out. To die at the hands of—' He lurched out of his seat and crossed the porch. 'To die alone.'

The numbness wasn't working. Wasn't doing its job. Pain for him leaked through and pooled deep in her chest. 'That just makes you human, Clint.'

He swung back to her. 'I'm supposed to be superhuman, Romy. Protector of the realm. I'm supposed to look out for others, not myself. I failed Justin, I failed that kid in the desert and now I'm failing you.'

'How?'

'I have an opportunity to be there for Justin. To make up for what happened to him when I was too busy hitting on some teenagers to watch for his safety. To make up for the slow start he got on education and how behind he was when our mother dragged him halfway around the world. I owe him that.'

Anxiety shook her voice. The stakes were just too high. 'Justin's made his own choices, Clint. As a child and as an adult. We all make choices and have to live with the outcome.' She glanced inside as though her outcome would come trotting down the stairs any second.

'He's my little brother, Romy. And he's in trouble. If it was Leighton wouldn't you do everything in your power to help him? Regardless of what path he'd taken?'

Leighton. The idea of her baby in trouble...

She sighed, knowing that Clint had no more choice than she did about who he put first in his life. 'Yes. I would.' Then she remembered something. 'But you told me yourself that part of every boy's journey is to stand on his own feet. Make his own mistakes. That I can't protect Leighton from everything.'

'It's not the same.'

'Isn't it?' Gut-deep sorrow sapped her courage. 'Maybe it's time for Justin to grow up.'

Hard as that would be for Clint to allow. Hard as that would be for her when it was Leighton's turn. Clint was a classic example of what happens when you can't let go. He was just too close to see it.

His eyes darkened. He pushed himself to his feet. 'I should go.'

This was it. The last time she'd see him. Anxiety surged up like a flock of birds exploding to flight. 'You're going to warn Justin?'

'I have to, Romy. Please understand.'

'I meant what I said, Clint. I can't keep Leighton here, near danger.'

He swallowed hard. 'I meant what I said, too.'

Talons tore through her. 'That I should go.'

'That you both should. Go somewhere that you can be happy. Where my darkness won't engulf you.'

Romy had lost too much in her life to let this break her. She stiffened her back, faced him and spoke between strangled breaths. 'You love Justin that much?'

Clint turned tortured eyes back to her.

She pushed. 'Enough that letting us go is easier than letting him go?'

Neither one of them pretended there wasn't something between them. 'It has to be. It's not about me.'

'What if he's not worth it?'

'He's my brother.'

And there it was. She'd been in his life mere weeks. What chance did she have against the boy Clint had spent a lifetime trying to atone for. Against family.

Romy stepped back and let him walk away.

Clint hated that this would be the memory he took with him for the rest of his life. The pain etched into the lines of her face, the confusion, the betrayal. He steeled himself against her scent as he stepped past her but it unravelled around his feet and tangled him, slowing him, wanting him to stay.

Almost as much as he did.

At the last moment, he turned and leaned into her warmth, pressing his icy lips to the furnace of her hair. Lingering. Knowing there would be no more kisses. No more sweet, natural Romy scent. She didn't want even that, pulling away violently and stumbling to the screen door.

And then she was gone. Inside, back to her family. He turned to go and find his. All that was left of it.

As he crossed to his ute, he forced the dark shadow down deep, where others lived and multiplied at will. What was more pain in his already bleak life? Getting his life together was a crazy fantasy. Men like him didn't get happy ever afters. He hadn't earned it.

The package—woman and child—would go to some other guy. Someone with more goodness in him. His journey looked a little different. But if he could salvage something for his brother, make good on years of separation and loss... That was a start, wasn't it? Worth something? But he couldn't do that with Romy around with her big, silent, all-seeing eyes reminding him every day of the monumental task that was going to be.

It would be easier alone. And eventually it wouldn't hurt this much.

If he was lucky.

Clint yanked hard on the door to his truck just as a word, high-pitched and desperate, screeched through the night.

'Leighton!'

It hung impotently in the air as he sprinted back towards the house and the wailing woman within.

'He's gone! His bed's empty.'

Romy burst out of the house and practically fell into his arms, her whole body trembling. Instinct forced him straight into field mode. He pushed her back and locked his eyes onto hers. 'Gone how? We were sitting at the doorway.'

'The window. He climbed down the outside of the house...' She spun around to scan the thick, endless darkness behind them and then called his name, loudly and desperately into the silence of night. 'Oh, God, what if he heard us fighting?'

'Then he's only a few minutes away.' The calm logic was nothing like the clenched fist of fear deep in his belly. He marshalled it in.

'I have to find him.' She turned and bolted back into the house and Clint stayed close behind her. Young boys and the Australian bush at night were not a good fit. His thumping heart went straight into a familiar rhythm. The rhythm of combat, the rhythm his mind was trained to work with. Beats that directed his thoughts, helped stop him from losing it.

With Romy falling apart he couldn't afford to.

But damn it, he was not going to stand by and do nothing while another child was in danger. His brother would have to wait.

He dogged her heels as Romy emptied the contents of her large rucksack onto the kitchen table. First-aid kit, water, torch, jellybeans for sugar, PDA. She hauled the GPS out, set it to track, tipped her head up to the ceiling and closed her eyes. It took a moment, but finally the unit returned a signal.

'You track Leighton?'

Wide, terrified eyes turned in his direction. 'I don't

have time for another lecture in obsessive parenting. I need to find my son.'

The unit started to ping, strong and relatively close. She turned the tracker towards the door and the pitch intensified.

'What's the source?'

'His backpack.'

Clever. Obsessive parenting clearly had its advantages. Finding Leighton just got a whole heap easier. No less dangerous but hopefully faster. She scooped everything back into her rucksack, slung it over her shoulder and sprinted towards the door.

'Romy, wait!' He barely managed to grasp her arm as she darted past him.

She tried to shrug off his iron grip. 'Go look for Justin, Clint. Leave me to find my son.' Her chest heaved with poorly repressed anger.

'It's dangerous out there for you, too, Romy.'

Her eyes seemed to soften and her body shifted slightly, alert but no longer—

The thought wasn't even finished and she broke free of his grip and ran. Man, the woman was fast when she needed to be. She was off the porch and halfway across the clearing towards the trees before he even got close to catching up to her. Did she even know where she was going? He kept his eye locked on the blue of her sweater. In seconds, it was swallowed up by the deep, dark green of the night forest.

He kicked into gear behind her.

Running full pelt through the darkened bush felt

strangely familiar. It reminded him of any number of secret missions in conflict hot spots, as though no time at all had passed since he'd been in active combat. He called on his training to regulate his pounding heart and lighten his footfalls so he could hear the bush ahead of him, follow his ears. Track his prey.

Crack. Over to the right.

He set off again, springing lightly on well-trained feet, dodging bushes and trip hazards in an effort to catch up with Romy. A big part of him feared for her. She wasn't used to moving through this bush and definitely not at speed. And her ankle was still not healed. There was every chance she'd hurt herself.

He kicked himself for caring. She'd turned his brother in without a moment's hesitation….

The pursuit ran on. Then, out of nowhere, a flash of movement caught his eye. She'd stopped running and limped towards him over to his right, shaking and gasping.

'This is not getting Leighton found, Clint!' Forming the words between laboured breaths was obvious torture for her. She favoured her injured ankle.

Clint toughened his heart against her drawn features, the brightness of her eyes. 'We should call for backup.' He couldn't bring himself to say words like *emergency services* or *ambulance*. A vision of another young boy he'd failed to save flashed in his mind. And another one, cold and blue from the water in a dam so close to here.

'You're my backup, McLeish. Help me or get out of my way.'

Choose. Justin or Leighton.

A grown man who'd made his own decisions in life or an eight-year-old boy who was desperately in need of guidance. Of a father. Of help.

Choose. Family or…

Clint's heart started thumping hard.

Somewhere in the past few weeks he'd started to think of Leighton as family. Of Romy as being his. The idea of both mother and son stumbling through the bush in the pitch darkness risking injury or worse brought a bitter, acrid taste to Clint's mouth. Romy knew a heap about surveillance but he was willing to bet she knew nothing about tracking.

His expression must have answered for him because a whimper of air pushed out of her. 'Let me go,' she begged. 'Let me find Leighton.'

'No.'

She stood impaled.

'Not without help,' he said. 'I'm coming with you.'

CHAPTER TWELVE

THE GPS locator led them straight into trouble.

The signal came from dead ahead but a massive granite outcrop blocked their way, looming and treacherous in the moonlight. Romy knew her wild-eyed panic was not going to help matters but she struggled to contain the fear.

Clint scanned the trees around them. 'This outcrop only goes for a few hundred metres but it marks a deep gully behind it. If we pick the wrong way we'll have to backtrack. Lose a lot of time...'

She swallowed hard. 'I don't know we have that much time, Clint.' She almost succeeded in keeping the quaver out of her voice.

'We'll split up. It's the only way.'

His decisiveness was comforting but the thought of continuing alone terrified her. She felt so much safer with him by her side. She'd faced some dangerous situations in her lifetime but none that filled her with this kind of horror. The *what if...*

Her baby had to come before her pride.

'Can we stay together, Clint? I don't think I can do

this alone.' Her breath shuddered as she inhaled deeply. 'I need you with me.'

That was a momentous admission and they both knew it. Regardless of what tomorrow would bring, regardless of what had just happened between them, right now in this moment she needed Clint by her side. Telling him felt less like an admission of weakness and more like a proclamation of strength. She frowned. In his eyes, triumph blurred with passion and something else.

He snaked his arm around her waist and pressed hot lips to her freezing ones. It was like a shot of air under water, filling her with strength and purpose. They would go on...together.

She looked to her left when he released her. 'What's that way?'

He cleared his throat. 'The lowland dams. But it's a hard scrabble in that direction. Let's take the right. It comes out on higher ground near the cockatoo roost site. He's more likely to have—'

Romy reeled back. 'The cockatoos! Oh, Clint...he's gone after the cockatoos.' She filled him in on their bit of detective work earlier in the evening. 'He's been rattling on about undercover surveillance lately. What if he's gone to check it out? He could be walking into anything....'

'Then we'll deal with it as it comes. It's a good lead, Romy. And when we find him—' not *if* '—you've been there so you should be able to find your way to the road and home.'

Home. With Leighton in her arms and Clint by her side. It was a bright, miserable dream. Except...

'Alone? Where will you be?'

He turned her back towards him. 'Romy, we don't know what sort of situation we'll find Leighton in. When the time comes, I don't need you second-guessing my instructions. That will only waste time and put him at more risk.' He took her chin and stared down into her eyes. 'I asked you once before if you trusted me. Now I'm asking again. To do whatever I tell you, no questions asked. Can you do that?'

She nodded.

'Say it out loud, Romy. You have to mean it.'

She took a deep breath. 'Whatever you think of my expertise, I've never doubted yours, Clint. I'll do whatever you say.'

The look he gave her would have crumbled the granite behemoth blocking their way. But there was no time to say more than a few words.

'Let's go get our boy back.'

Her throat was too thick to speak, so she nodded, blinking back tears. *Crying is not going to get Leighton home.* It was just like her father's voice but softer. More feminine.

Her voice.

Maybe it always had been? She tugged her pack higher onto her shoulder, turned to her right and followed Clint's courageous, broad back into the bush.

* * *

Within fifteen minutes, Romy's instincts were proven. The two of them lay crouched in the low scrub, peering out onto the clearing of the cockatoo roosting site, staring at three men and two vehicles. The GPS told Romy they were right on top of her son, but where was he? The doors to a blue ute hung open, affording her a view clear through it. No Leighton. Either he was in the white sedan or he wasn't here, only his backpack was.

She tried not to think about that.

Clint's hand slid over hers as though he'd heard her thoughts. He squeezed it gently and she flipped hers over and laced her fingers firmly through his. His strength anchored her just as she was getting ready to tumble away into panic.

His other hand rose up to her lips, his index finger silencing her, his line of sight moving to where the men busied themselves at the base of a particularly large jarrah tree. It was the best opportunity they were going to get. Whatever they'd taken Leighton for, their attention was well and truly off the ball now.

Clint drew her with him back into the trees. Her body resisted retreat even though her mind knew she'd promised to follow orders.

Hot lips pressed near her ear. 'Leighton's in the white sedan,' he said, and her round stare flew to the larger vehicle. Sure enough, she could barely make out the top of a shaggy head in the back seat. Her heart leapt.

Clint held her back. 'I'm going to create a diversion

and you're going let Leighton out and get the hell out of here,' he whispered.

Romy's eyes snapped back to his. 'I don't think I can—'

'You can do anything.' His focus held hers. 'You can do this. I will be right behind you. I won't let anything happen to either of you.'

The raw confidence in his expression infected her. She almost believed him. 'Okay.' She nodded. Then, more certain. 'Okay.'

He kept speaking, softly into her ear. 'Once you're clear I don't want you to look back. Keep moving until you reach home. Then lock yourself inside until help arrives.'

Help. Not *until I come for you.* But she'd promised not to question him.

He breathed in deeply, filling himself with her scent. To Romy, it was too close to goodbye.

He must have seen her refusal coming. 'I'm holding you to your promise, Romy. I know I'm the last person on the planet you feel like trusting—and after the things I said earlier, I deserve that—but it means I'm also the last person you should be risking your son's safety for.'

Lord, didn't he know he was the only man she would ever risk her son's safety for?

A muscle twitched high in his jaw and Romy realised how hard he was working to master his fear. She remembered something her father had said once, about courage. That it wasn't the absence of fear, it was taking action in spite of it.

She'd never met a braver, better man.

She nodded, suddenly determined to put on a valiant face. For him. 'We'll be fine.' She hoped her smile didn't look as watery as it felt.

His gaze burned into hers. 'I know. I can't think of anyone I'd have more faith in. I believe in you, Romy. I'm counting on you to get Leighton safely home. It's going to be scary but do it for me.'

Romy swallowed past the lump in her throat. As far as she knew, he was about to take on three potentially armed men with nothing but his bare hands.

I love you. She burned to say it. Knew she never could. Instead, she leaned forwards and kissed the corner of his mouth with her own trembling one. His eyes drifted shut and his hand crept up to cup her cheek. Then she smiled tightly, turned her focus onto her son and started moving.

Don't look back. Of course that was never going to work; but when she did, at the edge of the clearing, the edge of no return, Clint had already disappeared. She crawled arm over arm along the dirt until she found herself in the shadow of the white sedan. Every part of her was shaking with uncontrollable tremors. She heaved in a breath and hoisted herself to a squatting position, peering inside the rear of the vehicle. Her little boy sat crouched in the seat, hugging his pack and peering at the men out the opposite window.

Romy blew out slowly to ease her trembling and

tapped a whisper-quiet fingernail on the glass between them. Leighton turned his tear-streaked face towards her and she raised an urgent finger to her lips. His eyeballs bulged but he nodded and glanced nervously at the three men. So did she.

She remembered the game he and Clint had played down in Frog Swamp. She held up two fingers and made them walk along the edge of the window.

Can you run?

Leighton shook his head and lifted his feet. Oh, dear God. They were bound together with cable tie. She swallowed back the rage and bile and gave him a thumbs up so he knew she'd understood, then glanced around for any sign of Clint. It was like he'd ceased to exist.

Okay. Plan B.

She mimed turning a key and Leighton bounced enthusiastically and pointed wildly to the front of the car. She stretched over to peer in the driver's window, glanced down at the ignition and saw the keys dangling there. Her eyes rolled heavenwards.

Thank you!

She gesticulated for Leighton to put his seatbelt on and she eased the driver's door open, praying it didn't have some kind of audible signal. It didn't. She slid into the seat and fired the ignition in the same move. It turned over but failed to catch. The sudden noise drew six angry eyes in their direction. All three men started thundering towards her. Her hands shook so badly she nearly couldn't turn the key over a second time but at the last moment it caught and all eight cylinders roared to life.

A hundred black shapes launched like startled bats from the trees where the cockatoos had been sleeping. Romy floored the accelerator and swerved out of reach just as the first man got close enough to yank the back door of the car open. Leighton screamed and wriggled away from the gaping hole as the man tried to climb in. He kicked violently with his bound feet as the man got a hold of his ankles. Romy slammed on the breaks rather than risk Leighton being yanked out of a moving vehicle.

Out of nowhere a familiar shape crashed into the strange man and sent them both tumbling to the ground in a bruising tumble. Fists exploded in all directions.

Justin.

In her rear-vision mirror, she saw the third man disappear into the trees as though his legs were cut right out from under him by some silent wraith.

Clint.

And then there were none.

'Hold on, baby,' she cried as she slammed her foot to the floor, sending the sedan slewing sideways on the gravel track. She spun them around and headed hell for leather towards WildSprings's admin centre, spraying tiny stones behind her and wishing wholeheartedly it was a shower of bullets and not loose rocks that peppered the filthy men who'd taken her son.

Neither of them spoke as the white sedan sped away from danger. Romy didn't ease her foot off the accelerator until there was at least half a mile between them and the danger at Far Reach.

Then she glanced in the rear-vision mirror. 'Are you okay, baby?'

Leighton started to cry, compounding his fear with embarrassment. Her own relief played out in an adrenaline dump to rival any extreme sport Clint might undertake. Her whole body trembled. She finally got an understanding of why he liked his leisure time on the risky side. That kind of natural high would be a tough habit to kick. And given what he'd done for a living for so long, his adrenaline rushes must have been a constant, addictive feed.

'Shh…we're fine now, L. It's all over. You're safe.'

'I'm sorry, Mum,' he wheezed between sobs. 'I'm sorry…'

Romy slowed the car right down and looked at him in the mirror. She didn't dare stop. She'd promised Clint. 'We'll talk about it later. I'm taking you home.'

His gaze bulged for the second time that day. He stared past her to the track ahead and shouted. Romy slammed on the brake, sliding to a stop metres from where two cross-parked police vehicles formed an ad hoc roadblock.

The cavalry!

She killed the engine and leapt from the car. She sprinted towards Steve Lawson and a uniformed stranger, who both stood tense and ready, their weap-

ons drawn as she ran towards them. That fact barely
registered as she shouted, 'Clint! He's—'

'Romy, stop!' Steve Lawson's stern voice was barely
recognisable. She skidded to a halt. Just then his partner saw the anxious, eight-year-old face peering over
the back seat of the sedan and, without looking at each
other, both officers carefully lowered their guns.

'What the hell is going on, Romy?' Steve asked,
moving towards her and holstering his weapon. 'I got
a call from Customs—their agents will be here any
minute. We're the advance guard. Whose car is this
and why were you driving it like a rally pro?'

'Clint needs your help, Steve.' Romy kept her hands
out to her sides, suddenly uncertain because of the
unfamiliar timbre of her friend's voice—his police
voice—but took another step towards him. 'He's out-
numbered. His brother…'

It took longer than she meant to tell the story because she kept stumbling over a tongue thickened by
adrenaline. But she got the important stuff out, including that Clint had walked into a deadly situation
without a weapon.

And without knowing that she loved him. Anxiety
made her dizzy.

'Sarge?' Steve's partner called from beneath the lid
of the sedan's popped boot where he was carrying out
a routine search. 'You need to see this.'

Romy followed Steve to the back of the vehicle
where both men stood staring into it. Nearly twenty
light-bulb boxes lined a specially created holding case

fitted in the bottom of the trunk. Forty more were stacked empty nearby.

Light bulbs?

Steve gently picked one up and cracked open the box. A clutch of black feathers sprung free. Realisation hit Romy in the time it took to suck in a shocked breath.

Cockatoos. Young ones. The men were not after Leighton when they chased the car. They wanted the living, drugged cargo loaded in the boot.

Leighton was just in the way.

Their escape replayed in her mind—the man grabbing Leighton's ankle, not to pull him out of the car but to boost himself in. Clint's brother taking him down—despite the precious cargo—because he thought Leighton was the target, too.

Oh, Justin…

Steve cursed. 'Stay here, Romy.'

Both officers ran for their respective vehicles. They fired them up and surged forwards, around the stationery sedan and beyond it. She sagged back against the sedan, relieved beyond words that help was on its way to Clint.

How could she have left him there…?

'Romy.'

Her heart leapt and she turned towards the urgent voice as Clint emerged from the trees, breathing heavily and sweating. He slammed into her like a freight train, swallowing her into his arms and pulling her hard against him. His lips found the sweat-slicked skin of her hairline and glued there.

'Are you all right? Leighton?' His urgent words vibrated against her forehead.

'He's okay, he's in the car.' She tightened her hold around his waist. He hugged her back, nearly crushing her in his intensity. Her eyes squeezed shut. Home didn't smell like muffins or look like her cottage or sound like an eight-year-old boy giggling. It felt…just exactly…like this.

Romy never wanted to let go.

He pushed some distance between them. 'Romy, what happened?'

She stumbled several times, telling the story of their wild escape as briefly as she could. He looked at the car with narrowed gaze and then surveyed the contents of the trunk himself, never letting go of Romy.

'Clint, are you all right?' Desperate relief shook her voice. Every independent moment she'd ever fought for faded into insignificance compared to her sudden surge in awareness that he'd protected her. Protected Leighton.

That everything would be okay as long as he was around.

It's what she'd been feeling—and fighting—from the very beginning.

She *wanted* him to be in charge. Not because she wasn't capable of solving her own problems. She wanted it because he was so incredibly competent and she felt so treasured when he took care of her. When had she ever in her life been *treasured*? How was she going to walk away from that feeling?

Darkness crossed Clint's face as he turned in the direction the police had left. She touched his arm. 'Justin?'

'Tied to a tree. They'll find him.'

The air squeezed out of her. Clint hadn't helped his brother. Hadn't let him go. After everything he'd tried to do for Justin, it must have been like gnawing off his own limb.

She touched him again. 'Don't you want to be there?'

He swung blazing, certain eyes to her, slid his hands up to frame her face and leaned in to kiss her parted lips. 'No. I want to be here.'

His mouth was warm and strong and tasted like safety. Her body sagged against his, the terror of the past few hours finally catching up with her. He moved quickly to support her weight.

'I'm so sorry about Justin,' she whispered.

Clint brushed her sweaty hair back from her face. 'Don't be. Justin is not your fault.'

'He's not yours either.' Clint's eyes dropped away. Romy pursued him. 'Can you let yourself believe that?'

His lips tightened with his hold on Romy. 'No. I don't think so. Look at what he's turned into. Willing to exploit the birds we've given sanctuary to for generations. That's not the boy I remember.'

Never mind that he'd used his brother and their family property to effect his crime.

'I can't begin to imagine how much it must have hurt to see your own flesh and blood standing in that clearing....'

Bleak eyes turned back to her. 'I guess he hasn't been my little brother for a long, long time.'

A wailing siren drifted towards them on the evening air.

The birds... Romy twisted to look at the trunk.

He pulled her back around. 'There's nothing we can do until the authorities get here. They'll be comfortable enough there in the cool until the wildlife officers can check each one properly and recover them from the tranquilliser.'

'Why would Justin steal them?'

Clint's lips tightened into a straight line. 'Wildlife smuggling is big business. Every one of those birds could potentially bring $15,000 from foreign collectors who don't know or don't care how they've been sourced. To help pay off Justin's debts. It's a filthy, disgusting trade.'

Romy frowned. 'Justin's in debt?'

He sighed and nodded. 'I imagine I'm not the only person he doublecrossed in his life and I'm sure he was being chased by more than the authorities when he left the US over those drug charges.'

Romy swallowed, imagining Leighton living with the kind of fear his brother must be. 'Poor Justin.'

Clint stared at her, incredulous. '*Poor Justin?* Now

you have empathy for him? After everything he did. I saw him go for Leighton in the back of the car.' Disgust leached from his pores.

She pressed her hand to his heart. It beat way too hard to be good for him. 'No. Not Leighton. He tackled that other man. He helped us get away, Clint.'

A skirmish broke out in eyes dark with pain. His throat worked frantically. His chest heaved.

She touched him again, more because she wanted to feel him. 'He couldn't have known that Leighton would get involved. I think…I think he came good, Clint, when it mattered.'

Heavy lids hid his eyes and he kissed her temple, threading his fingers through her hair. 'This is all my fault. I should have seen it, Romy. If I wasn't so blinded by my own guilt…if I hadn't buried myself away from every living thing, then I would have been more on top of what was going on in my own property. None of this would have happened.'

She pushed him away, looked him hard in the eye. 'No. If Justin had made different choices, then none of this would have happened.'

'I endangered you both with my blind loyalty. The two people that I—' He stroked the hot skin of her shoulderblades under her sweater. Trembles butterflied down her spine. 'That was a choice I made, Romy. I chose badly. Again.'

'No. You saved Leighton. You saved me. I could never have done that without you. Justin may have been a thief but he wouldn't have hurt Leighton. Or me. I believe that.'

And somehow she did believe it. He was Clint's brother. Malice just couldn't run through the veins of anyone who shared McLeish DNA.

Tears sparkled in green anguish-filled eyes. She took a breath. 'Did you hurt him, Clint?'

After a silent moment filled only with the sound of ever-increasing sirens, he nodded.

Oh, my poor love... She swallowed. 'Badly?'

He cleared his thick throat. 'He didn't fight back, Romy. He didn't take his eyes off mine. He just stood there and took it until he couldn't stand up any more. Like he thought he deserved it.'

How long would it take Clint to recover from that? As if he didn't carry enough guilt.

Leighton suddenly shoved his flushed little body in between them, his feet unbound now and his glasses knocking sideways as he wedged himself, puppylike, between the two most important people in his world. Romy tucked him safely to her and held on.

Clint squatted next to the tearful boy. 'Hey, buddy. You've had quite an adventure, huh?'

The shaggy, auburn head nodded and Leighton wiped his running nose on his sleeve. Clint smiled gently. 'Why did you run away, champ?'

Silence.

Clint didn't let up. 'Leighton, why did you leave the house at night without permission? You know that's against the rules, right?'

The tiny 'Yes, sir' almost disappeared on the breeze. Romy was struck by how different this encounter would be if her father were undertaking the inquisition. Clint was taking no prisoners, just like the Colonel, but his methodology was every bit as gentle and compassionate as Romy would have been herself. Possibly more so.

As if he knew something about being a young boy who made mistakes.

The thought of a man Clint's size ever being a small boy made her smile. Then hard on its heels came another thought. About what kind of a boy they might make together. She shut down the tempting thought. Tonight's dramas would change nothing, long-term.

Clint's hand dwarfed her son's shoulder, sympathy and understanding in his eyes. 'Did you run away, Leighton?'

The tiniest of head shakes. Relief tightened Romy's chest. Believing her boy had been unhappy enough to run away had been weighing on her since she found his bed rumpled and empty and the window wide-open. Fearing that she had made him feel that way. How many times had she wished of doing the same thing when she was his age?

'Then, what? Why did you leave the house?' Clint gently persisted.

His words were almost a whisper.

'Out loud, Leighton. Your mother needs to hear this.'

Leighton dragged tragic eyes up to her. She itched

to bend down to him but Clint's warning gaze held her back. Now was not the time to treat her son like a child.

'I wanted to help, Mum. I wanted to catch the bad guys. To make you happier. To make you smile again.'

Not pulling her baby to her breast took all her strength. 'I'm not unhappy, Leighton. You should never put yourself at risk for me.'

'You've been so sad. Since we came. I heard you crying…'

A surge of heat raged up her throat. She glanced at Clint, whose eyes burned intently. It looked like anger but why would he care whether she cried her heart out in the darkness? She crouched next to her son and wrapped both arms around him. 'That doesn't matter now. I'm just so relieved everybody is okay.' She pulled Leighton into her body, kissed his head and flicked her eyes up to Clint's. 'There'll be no more crying, I promise.'

Awkward tension zinged between them. Romy opened her mouth to speak and then let it close again. The wailing of sirens grew suddenly closer.

'Saved by the bell,' Clint said, his eyes as vibrant as Leighton's green tree frogs. 'Unless we want to be caught here for hours yet, we should get moving. Leave the authorities to it. Steve will know where to find us when they're ready for a statement. Let's go home, Romy.'

They disappeared into the darkness of the bush long

enough for three official-looking vehicles to drive past them on the road. Then they clambered back up to the roadway and walked the long way home. At every turn, Leighton thought of yet another aspect of their daring escape to comment on excitedly. Romy knew there wouldn't be too many times that she'd hear the words *awesome* and *Mum* in the same sentence as he got older. She enjoyed the rare moment.

'Who's the hero now?' Clint murmured, swinging a finally flagging Leighton up into his arms.

They walked along in silence, Leighton drifting in and out of awareness. Conversation was almost impossible when so much needed to be said.

'You were amazing,' Romy finally said after Leighton had fallen into a deep sleep in Clint's arms. 'To put yourself at risk like that for Leighton, for us... Thank you.'

She burned to kiss him. Properly. Words just felt inadequate. 'You must have been extraordinary in the field,' she persisted, thinking of the way that man in the clearing had just...ceased to exist. 'A massive asset in combat.'

He adjusted Leighton in his arms, avoided her eyes. 'Every asset has an expiry date. After today I don't think I'd be as effective an operator.'

'Why not? It didn't look like you'd lost any of your skills.'

He stared at her, his focus burning even in the dim moonlight. 'I seem to have lost my heart for it.'

Her own heart started to pound again and this time

not from the rush of survival chemicals. This was fear, pure and simple. Opening this door just felt unsafe. She swallowed.

Courage was fearing it but doing it, anyway.

'I wanted to say…for you to know…that I saw tonight how important your training must be when you're in real combat. The way you knew exactly what to do—'

He stopped and turned to her. 'This *was* real combat, Romy. Just because it wasn't in a war doesn't make it any less dangerous. It was worse than warfare because Leighton wasn't some target to be extracted, just a name on a document. This was personal. This was our Leighton. I was struggling as much as you were to stay objective. That's why I lost it.'

'I think I understand now. It's not a choice you make. To turn the military on or off. It *is* you. It's in everything you do, every thought you have. It's ingrained as strongly as any value I try and teach my son.

'I've seen how you are with him,' she went on. 'I've seen the positive impact you've had on his behaviour. He respects you and your natural authority, Clint, and more importantly, he responds to it. It doesn't hurt him, it makes him stronger.' Her feet skidded to a halt as the ground seemed to shift under them. 'Oh, Clint, what if I've made him weaker?'

Clint turned back to where she stood rooted to the earth. 'Don't judge yourself like this. You've done a fine job raising him entirely alone, with no support.

There is nothing wrong with loving your son and not wanting to see him hurt.'

'Yes, there is. He needs to save me.' She sought out his eyes desperately. 'He put himself in danger to-night because he feels responsible for me. I was trying to protect him and instead I've made him think his mother is defenceless. That an eight-year-old boy has to protect his mother.'

The shock realisation doubled her over, the breath punching out of her. 'I did this to him, Clint! After everything I survived with my father, I've forgotten how to be strong.'

He lifted her face with powerful fingers. 'You're the strongest woman I know, Romy Carvell. You didn't want to raise your son the way your father raised you. That's entirely understandable. Everybody has a weakness. Forgive yourself that.'

'You don't. You're made of rock.' *One hundred per-cent reliable, bombproof granite.*

Disgusted breath hissed out of him. 'Nowhere near, Romy. I wallowed in guilt for a decades-old mistake, I ran to the army to avoid my parents' self-combusting marriage, I ran from the army when it got too ugly, I ran from death, and now I'm running from you. From what you and Leighton represent. It's what I do, Romy. I run. That's my weakness.'

She stared up at him, not caring if her heart was on her sleeve. Blood pumped, pure and hard, through limbs almost numb with cold.

'You're freezing. We should keep moving.' If it wouldn't disturb her sleeping son she knew Clint would have given her the shirt off his very back. They picked up the pace in an effort to warm them both up. Romy's heart burned like a furnace even as her extremities turned a light blue, and her lips, anaesthetised with cold, couldn't seem to stop moving.

'I should have waited before acting when I realised Justin was involved in the smuggling. I should have spoken to you first. I betrayed our...' *What did they have...a relationship? A bond? A friendship?* 'I betrayed you. I'm so sorry, Clint.'

'You owe me nothing, Romy. If anything I owe you.' He shook his head. 'You and Leighton have given me more than you'll ever know these past months. You let me into your family for a little while and I'll never forget that.'

You don't have to forget it, she wanted to scream. *Ask me and I'll stay.* With Justin gone, Leighton would be safe. She wanted them all to be safe. Together. She held her breath, waiting for the tiniest sign from the granite mountain beside her that he wanted her to stay. Wanted *her.* The night crickets and frogs chirped and croaked around them.

Endlessly.

Finally, her body forced her to breathe and the arctic inwards rush ached all the way to her soul as she realised—

He isn't going to ask.

She felt a strange warmth on her cheek and realised that the warmest part of her slowly dying body was her tears.

Romy barely felt the steps under her numb feet as she climbed up to the house. The warmth of familiar safety soaked into her chilled bones. Clint carried Leighton upstairs to his attic and Romy slipped his little shoes and glasses off and pulled the thick quilt up over her half-frozen son.

Leighton's soft hands came up to snag her sweater, pulling her closer. 'I'm sorry, Mum. I put you in danger.'

Oh, Lord...like father, like—

She realised the horrible mistake of her subconscious and shut the thought down. Clint McLeish was not her son's father and never would be. After the dramas of the night were over they'd still be where they were at the beginning of it.

Two damaged people who couldn't be together.

She took Leighton's chin in her fingers and stared fiercely into his eyes, hoping the emotion of her response would disguise the true origin of the tears that suddenly pricked. 'I would go into any danger for you, Leighton Carvell. Anywhere. Any time. Do you understand? That's what people who love each other do. No matter what.'

He smiled shyly and buried himself in her shoulder again for a final hug. Then he looked up at Clint, still half asleep. Painfully innocent. 'You came into danger for me, too, Clint.'

Romy's heart haemorrhaged for the blatant hope in the guileless statement. Her son adored this man. Probably as much as she did.

Her chest squeezed. Oh, there were going to be *two* very sore hearts when this was all over.

Clint stared long and hard at Leighton, the muscles in his jaw working overtime. His mouth opened, then shut wordlessly. He looked at Romy, deep and pained, and then something in his eyes shifted. As though someone had lit a lamp in a dusty, disused room and revealed treasures beyond belief. They widened as she watched.

He shifted his attention back to the drowsy boy below him. 'That's because I love you, too, champ.'

Leighton abandoned his death grip on his mother and threw himself against Clint. It was exactly what she wanted to do, but fear kept her motionless. Clint kissed the top of Leighton's shaggy head and then looked up at Romy.

She stared at Clint in taught agony and hissed, 'That's not something you say just because you think someone wants to hear it.' She nodded towards Leighton. But she was talking about herself. 'He's eight years old, Clint.'

'I know.' He kissed Leighton's head again. 'I do love you, kiddo. I will be right by your mother's side if you are ever in any kind of trouble and need me. Forever. I swear.'

Romy frowned her confusion through a pulsing headache. *Right by her side.* But that sounded decidedly *not* like forever.

It sounded like *forever apart.* 'You can't do this, Clint.' The ache hummed in her whisper. 'He won't understand.'

'He understands more than you know, Romy.' He shifted his eyes to her as he spoke, thick and husky and pained. 'I love you both. Very much. And whenever you need me, I will be there for you both. No matter where you are.'

The whole cottage lurched at her feet and her surging heart leapt painfully in her chest. She tipped her chin up and eyeballed him. Took a chance. The instinct to protect herself was almost overwhelming, but she forced the words from her cold lips. 'Why? Where are you going?'

He frowned. 'Nowhere. But after what I said earlier tonight…'

'You still want us to leave?'

'No! But—'

Her heart pounded. 'You want us to stay, then?'

His blazing eyes said *desperately*, but his voice was less sure. 'I've given up the right to hope for what I want.'

Thump, thump, thump. 'What if I want it, too?'

Everyone in the room seemed to hold their breath. Including Leighton. Romy stared into Clint's green eyes. She'd never seen them so naked. So brave. In the space between one blink and the next, she decided it was time she demonstrated some of that McLeish courage.

Screw fear.

'I want to stay.' The words wobbled, then grew more sure. 'With you.'

Nobody moved. Romy's heart beat hard enough to bruise her ribs. Then Clint gifted her with a brilliant, unrestrained smile and she was lost. She launched herself forwards, finding Clint's lips with her own across the top of a squashed Leighton.

'I love you.' *Kiss.* 'I love you.' *Kiss.* 'I love you, Clint McLeish.'

He kissed her back as though she was the very air he breathed, his mouth hot and hard and so, so gentle. Then his hands came around the top of her body and dragged her half across to his side of Leighton's bed. 'I've loved you since the moment you handed me all the things you stole from my shop,' he said, pressing his lips to her face, her hair, her mouth. She bit his bottom lip gently. Her voice was breathy, her laugh choked with tears.

'I've loved you since you completely missed me stealing them.'

He opened his mouth to protest and Romy took the advantage, covering it with hers and diving her tongue in deep for a hint of the heaven she'd been dreaming of since the night of the fundraiser.

'Eeeww, Mum.' Leighton pushed ineffectually against Clint's body. 'Gross!'

Getting out of her child's bedroom became a

necessary priority. She needed to be alone with Clint. They tucked him back in hurriedly and then tiptoed down the stairs. Clint kept one hand on her the whole time. Her shoulder, her back, her nape, her hip.

When his hand slipped up higher than her hip and his long fingers curled up around her rib cage as her feet touched the bottom step, she spun into his embrace. Into his waiting kiss. If the world ended now, Romy would go into eternity knowing she'd been loved. And more important, that she'd been able to love.

They both emerged breathless, laughing. Her body zinged with the same rush that flushed his.

'You asked me why I didn't want to go back out into the field.' He kissed her, slow and hard. 'I've got too much to lose now. Too much to get home to.' He kissed her again; she pressed herself to him. 'And I don't think I could stand to see that look on your face again.'

'What look?'

'When you thought you might not see me again. When I feared you were right. That's not somewhere I want to put you ever again.'

'You won't. I won't let you.' She kissed him, pulling him down after her onto the couch and leaning into him. 'I will never let you go.'

He smiled. 'Hey, enough of the stalker talk. You're creeping me out.'

She slapped him gently, then nestled in closer, looking at him steadily. 'Any time you doubt your bravery,

I'll remind you how you risked your life for the people you loved.'

'And right behind that, I'll remind you of your blazing brilliance as you rescued your son.' He kissed her soundly, then looked at her seriously. 'And rescued me.'

'You?'

'You have no idea the darkness and sorrow of the place that I've been, Romy. The day you walked into my shop it was like a beacon went off, bright and unmissable in the sky, and I've been guided by it ever since.'

'I wish I could give you a medal for what you did tonight. You deserve another flaming star.'

'Romy Carvell, I would rather just one of those glorious, lusty looks from you than all the valour commendations in the country,' he said.

'This look?' She threw her best movie-star come-on at him.

'Nope.' He kissed her until they were both breathless and then he slid his hand unapologetically up under her sweater. She flushed three kinds of hot and blazed back at him.

'Oh, yeah,' he murmured. 'That's the one.'

CHAPTER THIRTEEN

CLINT was respectful because the Colonel's rank commanded it, but the effort nearly broke him. He gripped the telephone handset brutally. 'Thank you, sir. Yes, I will. Goodbye.'

He spent a moment managing his pulse, composing himself, conscious of the grey stare blazing into his back. Then he turned to Romy, cleared his throat. 'Your father wishes to extend his congratulations.'

It killed him that she was too frightened to make the call herself. *Romy*. The brazen, bolshie woman who took on wildlife smugglers head-on, who stood up to Clint as though he were a schoolteacher and not a trained killer. She sat on the edge of his bed, still dressed in the white slip of a wedding dress he'd married her in, waiting nervously. Yet she still found room in her heart to care. Maybe to worry a little bit.

'How is he?'

'He's fine. He appreciated us letting him know about the wedding.' He pulled her into the protective cocoon of his arms. She was going to need it. 'He asked after Leighton.'

Romy stiffened perceptibly. He stroked her hair, whispered against her ear. Broke the news as gently as he could. 'He knew where you were, Romy. Almost from the moment you moved here.'

Fire broiled in Clint's gut. Not because the Colonel had tracked his daughter and grandson for the past six years but because of the impact that news had on his wife. She didn't tremble or stiffen further, but her skin went icily cold.

'The whole time?'

He kissed the delicate coils of her hair, lingering as though his lips alone could warm her back up. 'I'd do the same, Rom, if you were taken from me. I'd have to know you were all right.'

She clung to the sharp creases of his dress uniform. 'That's because you love me.'

He let her think about that. She pulled back, looked up at him with anguished eyes, shaking her head. 'No. He doesn't love me.'

'Not in any conventional way. I think maybe…in his own way… He just can't show it.' He let her digest the information for a moment. 'He sounds broken, Rom.'

Broken, but still a hard man. Clint got that after three minutes on the phone. Romy endured it for twenty years.

Her eyes clouded over and she pressed her body hard against his. 'I don't want to talk about him tonight. Not tonight.'

His arms came up to stroke the bare flesh of her

back, drifted blindly down to where the eagle stretched its wings over her hips. Where his code name branded her flesh beneath the softness of her dress. The shivers that Mexican-waved their way through her body suddenly had no relationship to thinking about her father. There was one sure way he could help undo the damage the Colonel had inflicted on Romy's gentle soul.

Love. In all its forms. Unconditional. Passionate. Eternal.

The familiar high rushed through him. But it was adrenaline of a new kind, the kind only this woman could elicit. He smiled against her flower-braided hair.

'Are you nervous, Mrs McLeish?'

She tipped her head back and lifted her chin, failing abysmally to be brave. Every Neanderthal instinct in him came surging forth, most of it mustering to his south. This was their first night together. Why wouldn't she be nervous?

Look at how her last experience had ended up.

The desire to plant *his* seed deep inside the woman he loved was so immediate, so primal and raw, he had to force himself not to sweep her up into his arms and make her his on the spot. He sucked in a deep, shuddering breath.

'I will never hurt you, Romy. As far as I'm concerned, this is your first time, as though you've never made love.' She met his gaze with a molten one of her own and his heart lurched.

'I have never made love,' she said. 'That's one hundred percent true.'

Clint dipped his head and kissed her, his fingers going automatically to the polished buttons of his military dress coat, his lips keeping his woman close. As soon as the jacket hit the nearest chair, he yanked at the strangling tie, burning up with the taste of her.

His shirt was the next target. Given it was the last time he'd ever wear his dress uniform, donning it for his wedding seemed appropriate. A symbolic transition between his previous life and his new one. His CO had been surprised to hear from him, but not surprised to hear he was retiring from the force as soon as his contract expired. With an honourable discharge, his reputation and his belief in himself restored, in order to focus on his family.

His new family.

The beige shirt fluttered down to join the coat and his fingers brushed Romy's trembling ones as they joined in removing his belt. Dangerously close to a part of him that was about as sensitive as a hair-trigger landmine right now. He sucked in his belly sharply as her fingers traced the definition of his obliques. Urgency made them both fumble. They'd been holding back for weeks, desperate to know every part of each other but determined to start their life together in a way that was respectful of her son.

Clint slowed to a halt at the power punch to his heart. *Their* son.

He smiled. He was a father. The wonders of this day were only just starting.

Romy peered up at him, her high cheeks flushed, her eyes the colour of stacked clouds during an electrical storm. 'Clint? You better not be changing your mind....'

Not a chance.

He captured her small hands in his and dragged them up between them, away from their dangerous play. It was no effort at all to spin her in his arms, and drag her against his body. The heat now flaring from the bare skin of her back soaked into his chest and his lips found the soft rise of her shoulders.

Romy sagged as she felt his lips press along the arch of her neck. Those magnificent hands gently encouraged the strap of her wedding dress down over one shoulder. Sheer modesty brought her hands up to capture the dress against her breast as the other strap followed.

'Let me see it, Romy,' he purred against her ear.

Delight whispered along her sensitised skin. She knew what he meant, what it meant to him. Knew he'd been extraordinarily patient. It was crazy, but there was no other part of her she was more shy about revealing.

'I want to see my name on your body.'

Clint's mouth was hot, wet torture as it worked its way over Romy's shoulder blades, down her spine and then followed the scoop of the fabric to his destination. He knelt behind her, his large hands reaching around to slip the dress completely off and let it fall to her hips, exposing her back and revealing her tattoo.

His lips traced the delicate artwork of the living raptor sealed into the skin of her lower back and her lashes fluttered shut. The scorching, sensual slide of his mouth over what had been her private shame was erotically charged and pangs of desire ricocheted through her. Her body curved like a marble statue, her head fell back and her breathing quickened as Clint explored the giant eagle, feather by excruciating feather.

Discovering his call sign was 'Wedgetail' had only confirmed what Romy had already known. They were meant to be together. She tore herself away from the sweet torture, kicked off her heels and scrambled across the enormous bed, sucking in desperate breaths, needing to put a tiny bit of distance between her and the blazing furnace of heat that was all hers.

Their hasty wedding date had been the scandal of the district but already the gossips were bartering something else—the arrest of Justin Long and the exposure of the smuggling ring.

Clint had seen to that. Her wonderful, capable, brilliant hero. Husband. He'd sacrificed his pride and privacy for hers. He'd also spoken convincingly for his brother in the preliminary court case convened a week after Justin's capture. The ordeal would stay with Clint forever but he'd done what he could to help his wayward brother. Romy loved him all the more for it.

She sank against the king-size bedhead, clutching

her slip to her breast and eyeing the mountain of a man she'd married. He rose back to his feet, predatory but exciting. She'd never felt safer with anyone.

He dispatched his footwear and trousers without taking his sights off her. Her heart hammered in her fragile chest. *This must be how a gazelle feels right before the lion strikes.* Except for her, the slow-motion waiting was a whole different kind of torture. The last time she'd seen his powerful body so revealed had been that day by the dam. Only there were no swimming trunks between them now.

She swallowed hard.

He stood, massive and strong, at the foot of the bed, looking every bit the defender of a nation. A wall of muscle tapered away from the smooth, round shoulders she loved so much—loved to drape herself off, loved to press her lips to, loved to feel under her fingertips. His body was a geometric work of art, all rigid planes and hard, defined edges. About as far from her ample, soft curves as possible.

Vive la différence!

He knelt on the end of the slab of a bed and crawled towards her, his smoky eyes locked onto their target with thrilling intent. Romy's mouth dried up completely. He stretched out beside her, lying on his belly on the covers, helping her to keep her wandering focus on the chiselled perfection of his face. His tattoo glistened beautifully on his tricep as he reached his hand out to tangle his fingers in the delicate silk of her dress. She touched the half-faded snakes, tracing their outline as he gently tugged the fabric down, away from her skin.

They drank in the sight of each other. The perfect contours of his body reminded Romy of their home, WildSprings. Hills and ridges of muscle, the gully between the curves of his glutes. She longed to explore every inch of that terrain.

She scooted down to lie face-to-face, burning to taste him, drowning in the green whirlpool of his eyes. He tipped onto his side and the energy between them reached out and breached the distance, twisting and tangling fire as though their skin actually touched.

'I love you.' Romy wasn't sure if she'd said it or thought it.

That made-for-kissing mouth started to move, its sounds strained and hoarse. She realised with a pang how hard he was working to keep himself in check.

'I'm terrified to touch you,' he growled. 'Of not being able to hold back.'

Her breath quickened. She reached out to place her hand over his heart. It thundered beneath its flesh casing.

'Why would you hold back?'

His straining voice matched the rest of him. 'It's been... I don't want to overwhelm you.'

Primitive power surged through her. She felt truly feminine for the first time in her life. She let her raptor spirit break free and locked her gaze on his with a bold promise. 'I'll match anything you throw at me. You can't break me.'

His body responded by tightening impossibly further. His sexy smile sent her pulse thumping. 'Didn't anyone ever tell you never to challenge a member of the Special Forces?'

Suddenly there were no nerves. No reservations. No past. Only this man that she loved and trusted completely. She slid her naked body hard up against his.

'So far, soldier, you're all talk. Let's see a little more action—'

If he was anywhere near as fast on the field as he was in bed, no wonder the military had worked so hard to keep him. In a flash Romy found herself on her back, a ton of rock-hard flesh on top and an acre of feather-down softness beneath.

His smiling mouth took hers.

Oh, this was going to be so *worth the wait.*